P9-DVO-303

# *Affections*

## Rodrigo Hasbún

*Translated by Sophie Hughes*

*Simon & Schuster*

NEW YORK   LONDON   TORONTO
SYDNEY   NEW DELHI

Simon & Schuster
1230 Avenue of the Americas
New York, NY 10020

Original text copyright © 2015 by Rodrigo Hasbún
English language translation copyright © 2016 by Sophie Hughes
Originally published in Spanish in 2015 as *Los afectos* by Literatura Random House
Published by arrangement by Pushkin Press

First Simon & Schuster hardcover edition September 2017

For information about special discounts for bulk purchases,
please contact Simon & Schuster Special Sales at 1-866-506-1949
or business@simonandschuster.com.

The Simon & Schuster Speakers Bureau can bring authors to
your live event. For more information or to book an event,
contact the Simon & Schuster Speakers Bureau at 1-866-248-3049
or visit our website at www.simonspeakers.com.

Interior design by Paul Dippolito

Manufactured in the United States of America

1   3   5   7   9   10   8   6   4   2

Library of Congress Cataloging-in-Publication Data

Names: Hasbún, Rodrigo, 1981– author. | Hughes, Sophie (Translator), translator.
Title: Affections / Rodrigo Hasbún ; translated by Sophie Hughes.
Other titles: Afectos. English
Description: New York : Simon & Schuster, 2017.
Identifiers: LCCN 2017004896 | ISBN 9781501154799 (hardback) |
ISBN 9781501154805 (trade paperback)
Subjects: LCSH: Germans—Bolivia—Fiction. | Families—Fiction. |
Bolivia—Fiction. | BISAC: FICTION / Literary. | FICTION / Coming of Age.
| FICTION / Political.
Classification: LCC PQ7822.H37 A4413 2017 | DDC 863/.7—dc23
LC record available at https://lccn.loc.gov/2017004896

ISBN 978-1-5011-5479-9
ISBN 978-1-5011-5481-2 (ebook)

# *Contents*

## I

## II

Although inspired by historical figures, this novel is a work of fiction. As such, it is not, nor does it attempt to be, a faithful portrait of any member of the Ertl family or the other characters who appear in its pages.

I

# Heidi

The day Papa came back from Nanga Parbat (with his soul-crushing footage, so much beauty wasn't human), he explained to us over dinner that alpinism had become too technical and that the important things were being forgotten, that he wasn't going to climb anymore. Clearly believing his words held some kind of promise, Mama grinned like an idiot, but she kept quiet so as not to interrupt. "Man's communion with nature is what really matters," he went on, his beard longer than ever and as dark as his faintly deranged eyes. "The chance to reach places God himself has forsaken is what matters. No, not forsaken," he corrected himself at the start of one of his interminable monologues, the ones he always gave when he got back, before the silence grew again, and with it the desire to set off on a new adventure, "but rather those places He can be found, where God finds solace away from our ingratitude, and our depravity."

Monika and Trixi hung on his every word, transfixed. Mama too, naturally. We were his clan, the women who waited for him, up until then in Munich but now in La Paz, where we had been living for a year and a half. Leave, that's what Papa knew how to do best. Leave, but also come back, like a soldier returns home from the war to gather his strength before going again. There usually followed a few months of peace in the house. This time though, having only just bemoaned the state of alpinism, and with his mouth half-full, he declared that he would soon be leaving in search of Paititi, an ancient Inca city buried deep in the middle of the Amazon rain forest. "No one has laid eyes on it for centuries," he said, and I couldn't bear to look at Mama, to see how short-lived her hopes had been. "It's full of hidden treasures buried there by the Incas to prevent the greedy conquistadors from looting them," he added, although these riches were the least of his concern. The prize he coveted was finding the city's ruins. It turned out he'd made a decisive stop in São Paulo on his way back from Nanga Parbat and finally had the funds and equipment to set off. "Let's not forget how long Machu Picchu went undiscovered," he said. "For hundreds of years, nobody even knew it existed, until bold Hiram Bingham came along."

Papa knew the names of hundreds of explorers, unlike me. I was one year off finishing secondary school and had other things to worry about, like what I was going to do afterward. La Paz wasn't so bad, but it was chaotic and we would never stop being outsiders, people from another world: an old, cold world. We had at least managed to adapt now, having struggled with every single thing at first, including blasted Spanish. Mama barely spoke a word of it, but my sisters were becoming in-

trouble. My other option was to go back to Munich, but the fact that Monika was considering this too put me off, because if she did we might end up living together. She had just celebrated her eighteenth birthday, had recently finished school, and was more confused and angry than ever. With her recurring panic attacks she had somehow managed to wangle it so that everything revolved around her even more than before, and Trixi and I had to resign ourselves to being minor characters, a bit like Mama in relation to Papa. I'm not going to deny it, it wasn't a pretty sight watching my sister having one of her hysterical fits. It was shocking, horrifying even. The last time we'd had no choice but to tie her up. Did Papa know about that yet? Had Mama told him in a letter maybe? Or earlier that day, before supper, as soon as they were alone in their room? Despite months of imploring by Mama, Monika just shrugged it off ("It's nothing," she would say. "Leave me be."), and she refused point-blank to see a psychiatrist or physician.

In any case, ten days after Papa's return, my sister's inner turmoil would coincide with another: the archaeologists from the Brazilian institute whom Papa was waiting for told him that they had to postpone the start of the expedition. He either didn't understand their reasoning or took it as a personal affront, and all hell broke loose in the house. Over the following days we listened to him make endless calls, slam doors, make threats, rant and rave. He spent the rest of the time brooding like a caged animal, like a man who'd lost everything. We girls were on school holidays and had no way of dodging this display of martyrdom. In the end, while Monika and I were helping him in the garden one afternoon, he suggested to her that she go with him. My sister didn't know if she wanted to study, or what or where she would study if she did. It was she who had questioned his decision to settle in Bolivia, complaining incessantly, even on the boat over. "We can't just up and leave our lives like this," she would begin, before really letting rip. "This is no way to do things!" "Not many people get the chance to start over," Papa would reply, and Monika would say, "There's no such thing as starting over. Leaving is the coward's way." Confronted like this, Papa would fall quiet and his silence gave her free rein to go on, at least until he lost his patience. When this happened Mama would take me and Trixi for a turn out on deck, and they would go on arguing, sometimes for hours on end. I would come to understand my sister's misgivings later, the day we arrived in La Paz. I recognized nothing in the city (there were children begging on the streets, native people carting great big bundles on their backs, too many half-built houses to count), and everything seemed unsafe and dirty. It was a couple of months later, with the family now settled in a central neighborhood and Papa having already set off for Nanga Parbat, that Monika's panic attacks began. That was nearly a year ago. Now, in the garden, to my astonishment she accepted his offer without a second thought.

Of course, Papa was trying to kill two birds with one stone: to count on Monika's help for the expedition, which he'd decided not to delay by a single second, and to put some distance between her and her demons. Having listened to him, incredulous, I declared that he should take me too. "You're still in school, you idiot," my sister cut in. "I can miss a couple of months," I told her, keeping my cool and promptly turning back to Papa. "This could be life-changing for me," I said, "you of all people know that." What must it have been like for him, coming home after such a long time spent in inhospitable locations? Was there something we didn't know that had made him want to give up climbing? And what was he really after with this business in Paitití? And me, what was I looking for? The chance to skip a few classes? To stand out among my friends and make them seethe with envy when I told them? Not to be left in Monika's shadow? As if he'd foreseen all this, including the questions I was asking myself, Papa pulled a strange smile as he nodded his consent. My heart froze in my chest and I looked at my sister, who looked at me, and neither of us knew what to say. I suppose it frightened us to learn that he was serious.

"You need to be prepared," he said after a while. We spoke in German among ourselves. On the rare occasions we were obliged to speak Spanish together, it felt fake. It was getting dark and we'd soon have to go back in. We'd finished weeding the garden—all that was left to do was to tie up the burlap sack and dump it on the street. "Materially speaking, we're more than ready," he told us. "We've got bite-proof suits, radio equipment, special cases to protect the celluloid, a terrific camera. We've got everything we need to reach the end of the world." He was able to buy all this kit thanks to the backing of a Bolivian ministry and the Brazilian institute, who had agreed to his setting off without their team. "The future is here," we'd heard him repeat over the previous days. "Europe had its chance and lost it. Now it's the turn of countries like this." He was no longer welcome in ours, regardless of the debt German cinema owed to him. During the Berlin Olympics, in the famous production by Leni Riefenstahl, Papa had been the first cameraman to film underwater and take daring aerial footage, the first to do many things. He'd also spent several years taking impressive photos of the war. Everyone knew about it, and no one better than us. Not for nothing had we moved continents and abandoned our life there. "Materially speaking, we're prepared," he repeated in the garden, swinging the burlap sack over his shoulder, "but not logistically, not yet. Nor physically or mentally, and even less spiritually." Did Mama know? Had they already discussed it? Would we leave without her consent? "It won't be easy," he said. "Nobody said it would be. Not for any of us, but we will find Paitití. Paitití has been waiting for us for centuries. We'll get there whatever it takes."

Three weeks later the new group had been formed and was ready to set off. Papa was the expedition's leader, of course. He wasn't an archaeologist, nobody in the group was, but that didn't matter, at least not for now. Rudi Braun had been on similar ventures (he was just back from Chaco), didn't seem tied to anyone, and knew exactly who Papa was, so he didn't take too much convincing.

He would be Papa's right-hand man, handling logistics. It took me all of two seconds to fall head over heels in love with him and thank my lucky stars that I was there. An entomologist by trade, Miss Burgl had been based in Bolivia for months studying some insect or another. She would help out in any way needed, and at the same time collect fauna specimens. Lastly, Monika and I would take on a countless number of jobs, including assisting Papa shoot the documentary he'd committed himself to making.

We traveled as far as we could in a Kombi. It crawled along slowly, perhaps because it was so overloaded. That first day we went through Balca and Chacaltaya, stopping every now and again so that he could film or take photos. He had shown us exactly how to assist him before we left, so we were already masters at assembling the tripod, knew all the different lenses by heart, and had a thorough understanding of the camera's various functions. We arrived in Sorata late in the evening and slept terribly, cooped up in a rented room.

The next morning there were twenty-five mules waiting for us and we loaded each one with packs weighing precisely forty-six kilos. Papa had warned us that any heavier and the mules wouldn't move. It was hailing and bitterly cold, ten times colder than the city. We had to cross the Cordillera Real at more than five thousand meters altitude. Our faces were frozen, and we were lugging great rucksacks on our backs. Breathing alone was a struggle.

Along the way we came across dozens of shrines, little piles of smooth stones carefully stacked in such a way as to survive the harsh climate. Whenever we passed one, the muleteers would scatter coca leaves around it and murmur prayers in Aymara. One of the muleteers explained to me that the shrines were there to honor Pachamama, the goddess of the earth, and to acknowledge the mountain spirits. I struggled to catch what he was saying through the round ball of coca he held in his mouth, a habit he shared with his fellow muleteers. They sucked on those leaves for hours on end. Apparently the sap gave them strength.

New mules awaited us at the summit. The muleteer in charge wanted Papa to pay more than the agreed amount on the basis that his people weren't happy, and the two of them wasted an hour negotiating. Papa mixed up his languages when he got angry, making it even more difficult to understand him. German, Bavarian, Italian, and English words all tumbled out together in a hopeless gibberish. I offered to interpret but he refused to accept my help. In the end they agreed on a figure, him conceding three thousand pesos.

A few hours later some sinister-looking individuals turned up, headed for Tipuani in the search for gold.

Papa's whole bearing changed in an instant, and Rudi, who had been bringing up the rear, moved forward to back him up. I shivered with excitement at his gallantry, or perhaps I was merely trembling at the wind that had begun to whip around us. We couldn't afford for any mules to fall behind. In an effort to help I counted them over and again, but I couldn't get past thirteen or fourteen without falling out of line, something that wasn't advisable given the conditions. Every now and then the bandits would ask questions, but on the whole they were unnervingly quiet. I began to imagine the worst (that together with the muleteers they would run off with our belongings, chopping us to pieces first), but half an hour later they wished us luck and drifted off in another direction.

It was getting dark as we approached Yani. The small adobe houses seemed to be piled on top of one another. I'd never seen anything like it. It was a bleak little village. The children roamed the dirt streets barefoot and with snotty faces. They looked at us as though we were ghosts and didn't return our hellos. How they didn't freeze to death was a mystery. Our problems came back to haunt us when a few muleteers and their animals disappeared. By the time we arrived, there were just six or seven of them. Papa went ballistic. The lead muleteer explained to him that his missing men had gone home for the night and would return first thing the following morning.

There was another argument and the muleteers were eventually summoned. Not long after that, the luggage was out in the yard, covered by a canvas sheet. The villagers skulked around, no doubt wondering who we were and what we were doing there. Papa became paranoid and ordered us to keep guard. Monika was the first to put herself forward, well armed with her air gun. Miss Burgl and I prepared dinner while Rudi and Papa disinfected the room where we would sleep. It had a dirt floor, in side, the walls were covered with old newspapers, some from as far back as the forties.

In the middle of the night Rudi woke me, stroking my head. "What's going on?" I asked. "It's your turn," he replied. "Ah," I said, springing up, elated to finally have the chance to talk. "Is anyone still milling around?" I asked. "Just two dogs that have been sniffing our packs for hours," he said. I wanted to believe he was smiling but couldn't tell in the darkness. "Get some rest," I said before leaving the room. A few hours later I woke up at his side, at which point I did see his smile as he wished me good morning. We were alone in the room. Outside you could already hear Papa ranting. On the wall, an article about the war caught my eye. I could recall very little from that time, and asked Rudi if he remembered more. He was tying his bootlaces and only replied that we oughtn't be late. He stroked my head again when he left, but more in the way one strokes a pet than a woman. It's possible he thought I was too young for him, or that he was scared of Papa, who, incidentally, insisted that day we address him by his given name. Hans, we had to call him, as we would a stranger—Hans and only Hans. Outside, the darkness was just beginning to lift and the muleteers and their chief were demanding yet more money. Was this what it would be like every day from now on? Did they take us for fools?

"For crying out loud be men and stick to your word!" Monika bellowed. An awkward silence hung in the air for several seconds before they all broke into laughter, even Papa, who ruffled her hair proudly as she too began to laugh. With that laughter the matter was resolved.

We set out again. Part of the route had been cleared centuries ago by the Incas. It was terrifying to think of it—it was fascinating and sad. It was all of these things too, to realize that we were lost in the heart of a foreign country, so far from home. The expedition had only just begun and it was easy to lose perspective, to forget that what we were doing day in and day out was part of a bigger plan, that all our efforts were directed toward finding a lost city in the rain forest. Paitití. I had to keep repeating it to myself like a mantra: Paitití, Paitití, Paitití. I was doing just that when I became distracted by Rudi and Monika's whisperings. On the days when she was in good spirits I envied my sister's lightness, her ability to make friends with anyone. I couldn't understand how her good nature could have such a terrible flip side. It didn't make sense to me that the sunny and the despairing girl were one and the same.

At nightfall we set up camp in Tolapampa. There was a stream nearby. The others didn't want to come with us, so Miss Burgl and I went by ourselves to take a dip. It was the first time we had bathed since leaving, and she was still a stranger really. She asked if my feet hurt. I told her I was absolutely fine, although the truth was my whole body ached. She asked me if I missed Mama. I told her I did. She asked me what she was like. "Melancholy," I said, a somewhat ridiculous answer, but I couldn't come up with another one. I was too embarrassed to mention the great balls of phlegm Mama had begun to cough up and which my sisters and I inspected as if they were newborn creatures. "We've got company," Miss Burgl said. One of the pigs belonging to the family putting us up was standing a few meters away, watching us. Later, when I relieved myself, it barely waited until I had left to dig into its feast.

I was awoken early the next morning by the sound of Papa rummaging around outside. Was it three days ago that we had left La Paz, or only two? And how much longer until we reached Incapampa, where we would set up base camp? There was so much to do I didn't even get the chance to ask. I had barely spoken to anyone over the first few days, least of all my sister. "Silence is key," Papa kept repeating. "Explorers know how to listen better than anyone, know to stay alert to their surroundings. Listening is just as important as looking, even more so," he told us over and again. Now, in the small hours of the morning, I could hear him pottering about outside the tent. Not long after, he appeared with a few plates of juicy sliced fruit and oats.

We were on the road again at seven, and by eleven a blanket of thick fog had descended upon us. Papa shouted at the group to concentrate and stick closely behind the person in front. Two muleteers near me began to talk in Aymara. I couldn't understand what they were saying, but their voices were relaxed and made me feel strangely calm. "We're heading down now!" Rudi bellowed. "Careful not to slip." I liked the way he spoke, firm and tender at the same time, unlike Papa, who was just firm. We were already wearing our green rain forest suits and the mounting humidity told us we were getting closer with every step. We looked like lost parachutists. We looked like soldiers searching for a war, or interplanetary beings. Every now and then the fog lifted and we could see the hills rolling out toward the east, covered by a carpet of trees that stretched out endlessly. Papa took every opportunity to film or take photos while the rest of us were forced to stop and wait, or to pretend we hadn't noticed the camera was on us, or to film him, who in turn pretended to not notice us as he got on with this or that. Somewhere down below was Paitití. I still repeated it to myself from time to time: Paitití, Paitití, Paitití. Rudi, I also said to myself. Rudi, my love. Rudi, my life. I had convinced myself he was single, but the thought of Mama made me accept that perhaps there was someone somewhere waiting for him. I don't know what possessed me to speed up even to the point of overtaking him, but as I did, a snake emerged from the undergrowth. Rudi threw rocks at it, sending it slithering back into hiding, and asked me to go back to my place. I couldn't even look at him for the next few hours.

We arrived in Pararani in the late afternoon and nothing there resembled anything we'd seen the previous night up in the mountains. The plant life was lusher and the floor covered in moss, the houses made out of the bases of tree trunks and palm leaves. The settlers were kind, friendly people. I was sweating profusely under my green suit. "Me too," Monika confessed when I told her. We set to work together, blowing up the rubber mattresses in the hut where we would be sleeping. If La Paz had seemed deprived up until then, these villages were ten times poorer. "You OK?" I asked. "Fine," she said.

"You?" "Yes, fine," I said. "Do you think you'll make it?" she asked. "As if it were even that hard," I replied. A few hours later, we were eating our dinner of tortillas and sauerkraut. Papa had managed to get hold of twelve men with machetes to help clear our path through the forest, and he seemed in good spirits. He told us that we'd reach Incapampa at the latest by two the following day, that it was a miracle we hadn't had any setbacks up until then, that he could already hear the hum of Paitití in the air. "What a good ear you must have, because I don't hear a thing," Miss Burgl said, and we all laughed.

That night I fixed it so that Rudi slept next to me. I gave him a kiss on the beard as I thanked him for what he'd done earlier with the snake. We were at the start of something, that much was clear, but we didn't know what. We were at the start of something and our only option was to go with it. Outside you could hear the buzz of the horseflies and swarms of mosquitoes. Rudi played dumb and didn't respond.

# Trixi

Papa and my sisters had been in the jungle for months, so Mama and I spent that Christmas on our own. It was the best one of my life.

I shouldn't say this, it was our little secret, but I will anyway: while we prepared dinner, I smoked for the first time.

It was Mama who offered it to me.

"Want a drag?" she asked out of nowhere.

I smiled. I was almost thirteen. Twelve and ten months, to be precise.

She seemed down, perhaps because we were going to spend Christmas alone. Even Paulina the maid had gone back to her village.

"Well, do you want one or not?" she asked again, holding out her hand, a cigarette between her fingers. They were bony hands. It was like seeing them for the first time. In many ways that Christmas was like seeing Mama for the first time.

"I started when I was eleven," she said.

It was hard to imagine her as a child.

I wasn't sure what to say. I wanted to try it and I didn't. I was nervous.

"In similar circumstances, actually," she added. "My mother got me into smoking too, as unbelievable as that might seem. On the shore of Lake Chiem."

I put it to my lips and inhaled deeply.

A violent cough erupted from my throat.

"You'll feel a bit dizzy, that's normal," Mama said, taking the cigarette off me and carrying on puffing away. She smoked with one hand, and with the other stirred vegetables in the pan.

It was already dark. No doubt everyone else was in their houses, with their families.

"You OK?" Mama asked.

"Yes," I said. I was.

"One more?"

I nodded.

This time it was she who put the cigarette to my lips.

I took a shallower drag, and the coughing started up again.

*Affections*

———

Mama was very talkative that night. Talkative because she felt like it, not because she felt she had to be, or because she believed it was her duty.

Maybe she was a little bit drunk too.

She must have been—she had polished off an entire bottle of wine on her own.

She didn't give me any to try. I would have to wait a few more years for that. She told me that life is longer than people lead you to believe, that at times it would feel interminable even. She told me to be suspicious of anyone in too much of a hurry to get where they want to be.

The moment she said this I thought of Papa and maybe Monika too. Heidi, Mama, and I were more absentminded, more careless.

We ate in the dining room.

Turkey.

And vegetable soufflé.

We laughed, imagining Papa and my sisters eating monkey, or snake stew, or any of those things they were supposedly eating now that their supplies were running low. Their messages were brief and we didn't always fully understand them, but we received word from them at least every ten days.

"I keep dreaming of Munich," Mama said. "It's as if I were living two lives: a waking one and a sleeping one."

"Which do you like best?" I asked.

We were at the table.

It seemed enormous with only us around it.

Mama smiled and took a sip of her wine. She had just opened a second bottle. Several seconds passed before she replied.

"I think I'm happier when I'm asleep," she said.

"I remember Munich too," I said, to make her feel less alone, or to get it off my chest, or who knows why.

"What do you remember about it?" Mama asked.

"Grandma's peach strudel, and the room they had in the hotel. We should go back and visit some time."

"If we go I won't want to come back," she said.

Out of all of us Mama had suffered the most. Since the move she could only really communicate with other Germans, but her health had also deteriorated. The high altitude in La Paz didn't agree with her.

I thought maybe I should go and give her a hug, but I stayed where I was.

It was ten or ten thirty. Still a while to go till midnight.

Christmas presents weren't customary in our house so I wasn't expecting anything.

We cleared the dishes, washed and dried them, and put them back in their places.

This was something Paulina usually took care of, on top of the cleaning, laundry, and cooking. She'd had to learn Mama's recipes because no one in our house liked Bolivian food.

"You're turning German," my sisters would tease her.

They also told her that we'd take her with us if we left.

Mama lit another cigarette.

She didn't ask me now if I wanted some but just passed it to me. It was the third puff of my life. Later that night there would be a fourth, and a fifth, and a sixth.

"I want you to remember me like this," she said.

"How?"

"Like this, Trixi. In the kitchen, smoking with you on the Christmas of 'fifty-five."


We went to bed without even putting on our nighties.

We were tired.

I liked listening to her talk.

I hadn't known that the first man she'd kissed in her life was Papa, or that Grandma and Grandpa had opposed their marriage, or that they'd disobeyed them and gone ahead with it anyway.

Rodrigo Hasbún

I hadn't known that before they had me they'd lost two babies, or that later they lost another.

"Would you have liked to have sons?" I asked.

Mama said she was happy with us girls.

"But your father would have liked to. That's why we didn't stop trying. I suppose in the end Monika was something of a son to him."

She let out a laugh as she said this.

"Did you fall in love with Papa at first sight?" I asked.

"The very moment I laid eyes on him," she said. "But I wasn't the only one. I think they all fell in love with him a little on the Olympic Committee."

I turned to look at her. Her eyes were closed and with one hand she balanced a glass of wine on her stomach.

I asked her if she still loved him.

She opened her eyes and looked at me.

I was worried she would tell me she didn't, but I told myself I'd understand. I told myself it was natural to fall out of love, that what was really quite unnatural was to go on loving. Or perhaps I didn't, perhaps it was only later I told myself that.

"More and more each day," Mama said.

She seemed to mean it, but I doubted her, because of how the evening had gone up to that point, how free she seemed suddenly, drinking as much wine as she pleased and smoking wherever she wanted in the house, and making me smoke and jumping into bed without even getting changed.

"It's late," she said, and downed her glass before putting it on the bedside table. Seconds later, when I turned to look at her, she was asleep.

# Reinhard

Yes, Aurelia, Monika's mother, began working at my parents' import business in May 1956. I remember it well because I stopped working there the same month. I had recently begun medical school and helped them out when I could. She was there the night everything went to hell between us. My parents and I could no longer bury our differences and it quickly descended into a yelling match. There were specific things I accused them of (they had a responsibility to their employee who had just been diagnosed with a tumor, the workers deserved better conditions), and less specific accusations thrown at me (my insolence, my naivety, my ingratitude), but what I remember most clearly from that last fight is Aurelia standing next to the till, caught in the crossfire, making out as though she couldn't hear our yelling. // Yes, I would later learn that Monika was the complete opposite, and that it is possible for such a meek and vulnerable mother to engender a daughter like her. But I didn't know Monika yet. Only by name, as Aurelia mentioned her in passing from time to time. Who could have imagined that years later her daughter would become so important to me? // Yes, there are people for whom one life is not enough. I often think this, in the darkness of my living room, glass of whiskey in my hand, at the epicenter of my new circumstances. How hard it is to bring together all the different people some people were, to reconcile, for example, the intriguing Monika from the early days with the impossible Monika later on. // Yes, my most constant thoughts, when the whiskey starts to take effect, are of her and only her, back in a period of much change: Monika in my room, reading aloud or ranting about this or that, or crying inches away from me. Monika in her early twenties, beautiful and ready to take on anything. Monika married to my brother but offering her true intimacy to me. I'm not ashamed to admit it: with a single look she could bring me to my knees. // Yes, when they hired Aurelia you could see she was bewildered, frightened even. It was clear she'd never worked before. My parents explained that she and her family were having some financial difficulties. I think she took the job to feel less alone. // Yes, for a long time I thought that Monika and I had parallel lives. We both arrived in La Paz in our teens, were both uncomfortable with that move and in ourselves. Back then we thought that made us special, that it mattered somehow. // Yes, a few years before we arrived, there had been a nationalist revolution in Bolivia. Despite making up the greatest part of the population, only then did the Indians gain the right to vote and to have their own land. As I understand it, though, this step in the right direction was little more than a smoke screen. By which I mean the Indians were just as fucked as they were before. Misery continued to be the norm for them. // Yes, the figures were shocking, even in La Paz, the richest city in the country. In the midfifties it had fewer than four hundred thousand inhabitants and sixty percent of them had never set foot in a school. The infant and maternal mortality rates were through the roof, and the sanitary infrastructure left much to be desired. Worst of all though was the continued existence of the criollo pseudoaristocracy, which a good number of the Germans and Jews arriving in the country joined. // Yes, it was during university that I began to lean toward the left and where I started to participate more or less actively in the meetings set up by the sociology undergraduates. I suppose they must have found my presence there strange at first. More than one of them probably suspected I came from a moneyed family. // Yes, Aurelia was uncomfortable talking about herself and I wasn't much of a raconteur. Despite this and the fact that we only overlapped at work for a few weeks, I felt an instant and genuine affection for her. // Yes, only a year or two later did I discover that she was already ill by the time she came to work for us. I wanted to visit her the moment I found out, but my classes and all the meetings were demanding more and more of me and I never found the time or courage to go. // Yes, perhaps if I'd gone I would have met Monika before my brother did and our lives would have turned out differently. I brought it up once, but conjectures irritated her and she immediately changed the subject. // Yes, after the row with my parents I rented a room close to the university and began working shifts in two clinics to support myself. I dealt with minor cases: healing wounds, looking after patients who thought they were ill but weren't. // Yes, away from my family and the conventions of my class I leaned farther and farther to the left and was soon making ties with student leaders. We often met up in my room, and it was there too that I became a man, although it's also true that the Bolivian girls were pretty chaste. // Yes, even now, whiskey in hand I invariably get stuck on the past and on Monika, who showed up soon after and for me encapsulates those years better than anyone: Monika furious or euphoric, questioning everything, Monika licking or kissing or moaning or simply still, the woman she was before becoming the woman she became. Out there on the other side of my window La Paz is nowhere to be seen. In here, on this side, is a bearded, balding man, no longer that young, grateful boy. // Yes, there was little love lost between me and my brother, and our estrangement was easy and gradual. Monika didn't have anything to do with it. // Yes, she's the only one who matters now, the misunderstood child, the chaotic, rebellious teenager, the woman who went on to lose all perspective and no longer knew when to stop and ended up hurting herself and others. // Yes, if you pressed me, I would say this is the definition of her that sticks: the woman who went on to cause so much hurt.

# Heidi

The second half of the expedition, in which I wasn't allowed to take part, was coming to an end, and Mama and I went to catch up with Papa and Monika, Miss Burgl, and Rudi.

The journey was torturous, especially for Mama. I never heard her complain so much—at night her back was agony. Traveling by mule isn't easy. A couple of hours in and you start to ache down to your soul. I gave her firm massages, brutally firm, but even then she asked me to put all my weight on her, to squeeze harder.

Now she was sitting next to Papa and nothing in her behavior suggested how unbearable the last three days' traveling had been. I was sitting next to Rudi, which made it tricky to look at him. I did anyway, and every now and then asked him for the salt or pepper. He had lost weight and let his beard grow almost as long as Papa's, but there was another, more drastic development: he seemed more absent than before. The same went for Monika. Seeing me and Mama hadn't cheered her up in the slightest. Papa was the only one who seemed unchanged. With that unflappable conviction of his he explained how they had uncovered two carved stone funeral terraces, three walls, and a lookout, but that they weren't sure yet if they were part of a larger construction or not. He told us they had a gold mask, three sacrificial knives, and various vessels, all now safely stored away, and that these objects held the key to an ancient culture. As if that weren't enough, he added, they'd caught some spectacular scenes on camera. It wasn't an easy subject to broach, but I did anyway: I asked about Paitití. A strange silence fell over all of us, even those who hadn't been talking. "We'll need more time to get there," Papa said at last. "Nothing can be gained from one or two trips. Or rather a lot can be gained, like coordinates for future expeditions." "Well, you can no longer count on me," Monika interjected, I'm not sure if in jest or seriously, but neither Mama nor I could help laughing.

This emboldened Monika to tell us the story of Luisa and Felipe, the cock and hen that had accompanied them throughout the expedition. "The second half of the expedition," I wanted to correct her, but didn't dare. They were given the chickens by an old lady from Huaricunca whom they'd come across along the way. I noticed Mama was resting her hand on Papa's knee and this cheered me up. I also saw, out of the corner of my eye, Rudi absorbed in his food. "The old lady's eyes were seeping pus," Monika said. "The poor woman could barely see and still she helped us." "We washed her eyes with boric acid," Papa added, "and left her a tube of penicillin to apply to them." "We went on our way thinking we'd never see her again," Monika continued, "but fifteen days later she showed up here." "She was hunchbacked, could barely walk," Miss Burgl chimed in for the first time since we'd sat down at the table. It annoyed me to note a kind of complicity among them all, to feel I had stopped being part of the group. I had hated every moment of those eleven months of separation, having had to go back to school instead of staying on with them. "That's right," Monika went on, "she could barely walk, but two weeks later she reappeared with healthy eyes, bringing us Luisa and Felipe as a thank-you." "Do you realize how far she walked?" Papa asked. "How far?" I asked. "At least four hours here and another four back," Papa answered. "Her village is past Maripi." "She walked painfully slowly, leaning on a stick," Monika said. "It was wretched to watch." "The point," Papa said, "is that this brave old woman shared many of the legends about Paitití with us. And what's more, she came back to see us every fortnight. It was she who told us how the Inca gods put a plague of fire ants and snakes over the region to protect it." According to Papa this wasn't the only thing the gods did. He explained to us that they also put an invisible veil over Paitití, invisible to the eyes of those hungry for riches. "Well, it's a legend," Miss Burgl interrupted again. "Which doesn't mean to say it isn't based on truth," Papa said. "Anyway, according to the old woman the veil only affects greedy types, the ones who come in search of material treasures." "The cock and hen were lucky charms," Monika intervened. "The old lady promised they would look after us. You can't imagine what these two are like when there's a snake nearby," and she laughed, as did Rudi, to my surprise and dismay. They had remembered something I wasn't privy to.

I withdrew from the conversation for a second and imagined us as characters in one of those films I sometimes watched with my school friends. We weren't a normal lot, to say the least, especially when Papa started doing his impression of the hen. "How did the old lady know where to go?" Mama asked a little while later. Clearly she was still thinking about the woman, about her ordeal, about the ordeal she and I had gone through to get there. "Telepathic faculties aren't rare among these people," was Papa's answer. I waited for him to chuckle after he said it, but instead he just went on eating as if it were nothing. I admit: I told myself at that point that he was losing his mind, or that he'd already lost it, that the gap between his delusions and reality was becoming wider. To distract myself I inched my leg toward Rudi. He drew his away. Mama proposed we drink the *singani* we had brought along with us. She served it and we toasted everyone's being together again. "Everyone apart from Trixi," Mama hastened to add, no doubt feeling guilty for having left her at home with the maid. It was too long and grueling a journey for us, let alone a little girl. There had been no other option. "Let's raise a toast to the end of the adventure too," Miss Burgl said. "Not to the end," Papa said, "a toast to its beginning," and he took a sip from his glass and we drank from ours.

I asked Rudi where the other men were and he answered that they'd left weeks ago for Tipuani to do some gold washing. "And Julio Durán?" I asked. He was the muleteer who had helped me and Mama and our five overloaded mules. "Resting," Rudi said. Getting him to speak was like drawing blood from a stone, at least when my parents were around. Maybe something had been lost between us. It wouldn't be long until I was of age, and then there would be no excuse. "What will you do after?" I asked. "Once we're back?" he asked. I nodded, nervously. "Go to Bremen for a while," he said. His lack of interest was hurtful. I thought how easy it is for people to grow apart, how easy it is to lose people. Had he changed so much? Or was it the way I saw him that had changed? "Back in a bit," I said before getting up and walking off to a nearby clearing. I wanted Rudi to come after me, wanted to kiss him passionately the way you see in films. I had spent months imagining it. I wouldn't say a word, just walk up to him and kiss him, with tongues and everything.

In fact it was Monika who appeared a few minutes later. She asked if I was OK. I nodded. "You?" "Yes," she said, "but I'm sad all this is coming to an end." "Well, it's not over yet," I told her. "It will be in a few days," she said and sat down next to me on a tree trunk. In the rain forest trees sometimes fall of their own accord, just drop down dead from one second to the next. We sat in silence, not knowing what else to say. Since Mama and I had joined them I'd had the chance to observe her more closely. She was rather sunburned and her arms were covered in small red *marihui* bites, but apart from that she looked the same. I wondered if she'd had more panic attacks, if she'd reaffirmed her vocation as an adventuress, if she'd calmed down for good. "I couldn't imagine myself in the city again," she said after a while. "Sometimes that scares me. This stillness is deceptive." "Don't be so dramatic," I replied. Monika flashed the hint of a smile. "Are you serious you don't want to be part of the next expedition?" I asked. "There won't be another," she said. "But Papa said that this has just begun." "I doubt that, and anyway, didn't you hear him? Paitití is invisible to strangers," she added, laughing to herself. "Mama is happy to be here," I said. "The whole way she joked that finally she'd get to see her husband's office." "It's a magnificent office," Monika said, "there's no doubting that."

We had a hug before heading back to camp. Perhaps it was our way of acknowledging the distance between us, our way of telling each other the things we didn't know how to say.

The next day Papa took Mama to see the ruins, or what he insisted on calling the ruins. I decided to leave them to it and hang back at camp. Miss Burgl took the opportunity to show me her collection of butterflies and snakeskins, a few of which were unimaginably beautiful—black and green and purple and bright orange. "This Yoroma is my favorite," she said. "It's not poisonous. Not all snakes are." She told me they'd long since stopped being afraid of them, even the ones that hung from the trees, which weren't usually hostile. "Ah, and look at this," Miss Burgl said, passing me a jar containing a bird I'd never seen before, its wings specked with vivid red. "These are the Incas' sacred birds, *tunkis*," she said. "Can you even

imagine how much destruction they must have seen?"
"And what are these?" I asked, pointing to another jar.
"Tucandeira ants," she answered. "Your father filmed a
breathtaking scene with hundreds of them gorging on a
mule we lost." What must Mama and Papa be doing in
the middle of the forest? Kissing passionately, the way I
wanted to kiss Rudi? It was for both these reasons—so
that they could kiss in peace and so I could try to kiss
Rudi—that I'd stayed behind. Monika was still asleep
and I hadn't seen Rudi anywhere. "So have you finished
school now?" Miss Burgl asked me. "Yes," I said, and
I knew what was coming because everyone had been
asking me the same question, so I beat her to it and told
her I wasn't sure what I wanted to do next, but that one
possibility was to go to Bremen. "To Bremen?" "Yes," I
said, without elaborating. "I've got arachnids too," she
said. "Want to take a look?" She appeared suddenly to be
an overgrown child, just like Papa the day before: a boy
who couldn't or didn't want to grow up. "How old are
you?" I asked. "Twenty-eight," Miss Burgl answered,
and she peered at me. "Why?" "Haven't you ever been
married?" She shook her head and her lips formed a
smile. "Do you worry about that?" she asked. "No, not
at all," I replied. "You're still very young," she said.
"You've no need to worry about that." "It doesn't worry
me," I insisted. "Here they are," she said, taking vari-

ous jars filled with formaldehyde where different types of tarantulas lay, trapped in time. "Fascinating, don't you think?" "Yeah, I guess," I said, beginning to lose my patience. "And Rudi?" "He went with the guide to pick up the equipment from the other camps," Miss Burgl said. "They left early." She must have read something on my face because she asked me if I wanted to go for a swim in the river.

"These last few months it hasn't stopped raining," she told me when we got there, taking off her clothes. "There's nothing quite as amazing as tropical rain. From one minute to the next the heavens open and it just comes crashing down," she said. "But in the end I have to say it wore us all out." For some reason, this time I was embarrassed to get undressed. Miss Burgl was already soaping her arms and legs. I couldn't help but look at her thick pubis and her little breasts, at her almost translucent skin. A few butterflies began fluttering around my clothes, which I'd left to one side. "They like filth," she said. "Who would have thought it, eh? So beautiful, and the thing they love most in the world is filth." The water only felt cold for the first minute or so. Miss Burgl passed me the soap and I rubbed it over my chest. What if Rudi saw us? Which of our bodies would attract him more, mine or Miss Burgl's? Had something gone on between them? I thought about him all the time. He was becoming an obsession, a constant companion, white noise in my head. "Will you take part in the next expedition?" I asked. "I don't think there'll be a next one," she answered. "Papa said there would be," I said. "I'll go if there is one," she said, "but I don't think there will be."

We washed our faces and hair, then relaxed. I closed my eyes, focusing on the sound of the forest and trying to hear the beating of my own heart. It felt good to be back, if only for a few days. It felt good to know that for tens of kilometers around us there was no one else, just Papa and Mama kissing (or probably not, why go on kidding myself?), Rudi and Julio Durán collecting the remaining equipment from the other camps, Monika sleeping, thousands of animals getting on with their animal lives. Would I end up leaving to avoid losing Rudi? Would Monika go too? What would it be like to live alone with her, shrinking ever smaller in her shadow, feeling uglier and stupider and less funny and less interesting than my sister?

Ten minutes or so later, Miss Burgl asked me if I'd ever met Leni. The question took me by surprise. "Leni Riefenstahl," she added. "Do you know who I mean?" "My father worked on lots of her productions," I replied. "He was one of her cameramen, her star cameraman." "I know," she said, "but what I asked was whether you had met her." I could have asked her why she wanted to know or what had made her think of Leni. "Yes," was all I said, "but I was still a little girl then really." "And your mum?" Miss Burgl went on. "What about her?" "Was she a friend of Leni?" "No idea," I replied, "you'd have to ask her yourself." But the second I said it I realized that I had never once seen Miss Burgl and Mama speaking.

We fell silent again after this. I could have stayed there in that water forever. Five minutes later we got dressed and left. There was lunch to be prepared before the others got back.

Everything was ready by seven the next morning and both Mama and I had been instructed as to the exact framing Papa wanted. Unlike Mama, I was familiar with the camera and lenses and wasn't fazed. It was a decisive scene, the dramatic ending to the documentary that Papa had spent months searching for. But what we were about to do wasn't only for the sake of the scene, he said. It would also clear the land, leaving it ready for the real archaeological mission to come.

Papa had just two more weeks to get all of the filmed material to São Paulo, at the start of June. Julio Durán told him that given the interminable rains they'd had, they would need a dry spell of at least three months for the plan to work properly. Papa wasn't prepared to hang

around, hence he had asked Mama and me to bring dozens of cans of combustible oil with us. The others opened
them and poured their contents all over the valley, us
filming them. Then, from various different points, they
started the fire. Very quickly the flames began to give off
a dark smoke, and you could hear the animals' cries. A
flock of parrots took flight and several vultures appeared.
They circled us from above and dived down into the fire,
reemerging with animals clutched in their talons. Chaos
reigned — it was a terrifying spectacle.

Papa gave us the signal to film him and the others
as they fled the fire. Then racing back toward us, he
snatched the camera back to take some extra footage
while the rest of them celebrated the great destruction.
Monika and Miss Burgl began to cry, or perhaps it was
just sweat on their faces. I saw my chance and took it,
throwing my arms around Rudi, and for the first time I
knew he wanted me too. Our embrace didn't last long. It
quickly became clear that the wind had changed direction
and we were forced to race back to the camp.

What had been the hired workers' lodging was now
ablaze on one side. Rudi and Julio Durán ran to take the
luggage we'd stored in there, while Papa tried to capture
the moment on camera. He ordered the rest of us to take
what we could to the river. Miss Burgl grabbed the cock
and hen, and Monika, Mama, and I took the sleeping bags

and a few provisions. The fire had now taken the entire hut and was spreading to the dining area. All whipped up, Papa asked Mama and me to film him and Monika soaking a few tarpaulins in water and spreading them over the tent where Miss Burgl kept her specimens. My sister didn't seem afraid of the fire. I was impressed by the precision of her movements.

A roar of thunder stopped us in our tracks. Papa, Rudi, and Julio Durán looked up to the sky and it was all caught on camera. As if planned, the heavens opened, fighting the fire from above. Papa began to shout with a euphoria that made me shudder, and for a few seconds I felt afraid of everything: of what we didn't know (considerably more than what we knew), of what each of us held inside us, of everything outside the present. Above all, I was afraid to feel so afraid. But there was no room for error and I told myself to pull it together and focus.

Papa was now the only person in the frame. The others had gradually slowed to a standstill. He yelled like a man possessed, his arms stretched up to the sky. The rain was drenching his hair, beard, and clothes. "Thank you!" he shouted. "You're there! I see you! Thank you, you goddamn son of a bitch!" He didn't seem to notice he was the only one still celebrating. And then the celluloid ran out and the camera stopped filming.

# Monika

You marry a man with the same name as your father and this doesn't amuse you. Your father isn't there to shake his hand or to hug you, to offer you up with these gestures to the man who will take his place. At your own wedding, at least for a couple of seconds, you feel like the loneliest woman in the world. All women must feel this at their weddings, you think, in an effort to console or merely distract yourself, or perhaps to do both things at once. Trixi is the only one there with you. That afternoon your family has been reduced to her alone, and there's something heartbreaking about this basic realization, but also something incomprehensibly liberating. Until recently, you thought that you would never do it, that marriage wasn't for you. Months after meeting him, perhaps believing in the promise of a different life, one unremarkable Saturday you get married.

———

On the wedding night he can't get an erection. You see him naked for the first time—his sinewy body, his long, slim dick, the scar from his peritonitis operation—and feel not a hint of excitement or conviction. Is this a typical wedding night? He touches you all over with his soft, rich kid's hands. He licks your nipples and neck, kisses you clumsily either in desperation or impatience, perhaps fearing you or himself, but he can't get an erection, not even when you stroke him. You wonder whether he might still be a virgin, whether perhaps he's only ever been with whores, whether it isn't women he's into at all, whether he, like you, doesn't understand why he got married. You wonder what your parents' wedding night must have been like—it's always been beyond you to imagine them young. You think about how your children won't be able to imagine you. "You're distracted," your husband says. He's a silent man, he knows how to observe himself at a distance. It's the thing you most admire in him, perhaps the only thing you admire. Despite what you always believed, it's something you have forgotten how to do. You feel too close to yourself, and from there everything looks blurred. "No," you tell him, "I'm not."

———

Trixi helps you move your clothes and belongings and to arrange them in the space your husband has made for you. Your husband: strange to say and strange to think it, but that is what you call him in your head, because he shares his first name with your father, and that is stranger still. Your sister only has two more years of school to go. She is no longer a little girl and has turned into a nervous creature, beset by tics. It occurs to you that she would be very easy to sum up: she's an oddball. Is this her way of occupying the things that upset her? Her way of protecting herself from what she doesn't understand or might hurt her? Is entering into marriage with a rich kid with soft hands your way? Would you also fit into a single phrase: the one who got married to escape? Escape from what? Hadn't you had relatively happy lives, at least up until a year ago when your mother's health really began to deteriorate? Is it from that irrevocable deterioration and outcome that you're trying to escape through marriage? Or from the distance that's grown between you and your father? And why won't you call a truce now that you're settling your things into a new room, supposedly at the start of something, the dubious start of a different life? You tell Trixi about your wedding night. She just laughs. "I don't know what to say," she says, and you realize she is more naive than you thought. It does you good talking to her. Her presence does you good. You ask if she's seeing anyone (she shakes her head), if she has any idea what she'll do after school ("I've still got two years to go!" she laughs), if she has heard anything from Heidi or Papa (she shakes her head). Hours later you hug good-bye at the gate. "Poor thing, how will you ever get used to such luxury?" she teases. Walking the thirty meters back to the front door takes you don't know how long. As you walk, you imagine the house as a prison.

Despite having done everything in your power to avoid it, you will live for a time with your parents-in-law. His father is a cordial man, his mother offhand. She takes every opportunity to show you she disapproves of her son's choice, that she had hoped for someone different for him, someone more refined and submissive, less ungrateful. You've already gone through their bedroom, the storeroom, living room and kitchen, but nowhere did you find anything remarkable. The house and the lives of those who inhabit it lack any mystery at all. You, on the other hand, hold on to just a few mementos from your past life: the expedition diaries, some old letters, no more than ten photos, and that's it. You avoid going through them. The last thing you want is to get stuck on places that no longer exist, and the photos and diaries and letters are themselves reminders that they don't. Better to hide them—perhaps you should even get rid of them. That would be the most logical and appropriate thing to do, the thing that would help release you from it all. You don't do it, however, because you still can't bring yourself to. In the evenings, after interminable meals with his parents, you tell your husband that the situation makes you uncomfortable and that you should start looking for a house together at once. "What situation?" he asks as if he hasn't noticed, ~~searching out your body under the sheets, fondling your~~ nipples, your neck and hands, arousing neither you nor himself, and promptly giving up to think about something else—his whores, his homosexuality, his work. "This situation," you say. "We didn't get married to go on being children."

Because it behooves you living in such a poor country, because you can't stand being in the house with his parents, because some days are too far from what you imagined for your life, you decide to set up a shelter for the needy with Lilota. You've known her since your first day at school in La Paz (when you couldn't speak more than twenty words of Spanish, it was she who kept your head above water), and you've been friends ever since, for five years now, although at times you think

you don't know the first thing about each other. Lilota
is still unmarried and gets fatter by the day, neither of
which things seems to bother her. She's excited at the
prospect of starting up a project like this together. Your
mother-in-law and her friends are experts in all things
charitable and give you advice. What drives these mis-
erable old women to go to such lengths to help other
people? you wonder as you listen to them. What moves
them to these shows of solidarity if in their day-to-day
existence the only thing they seem to care about is their
own comfort? Is it, in fact, nothing but show? In the
following weeks, you meet with businessmen and trad-
ers, bankers and lawyers, all German or the children of
Germans, and you pull together eighteen thousand dol-
lars, including the five thousand your husband throws
in. You're surprised by your own powers of persuasion,
and delight in taking charge. Thanks to your determination, two months later the shelter is up and running.
Was this what becoming an adult was? Making decisions
and taking responsibility for the things you do or stop
doing? Was being an adult assuming that there is no
longer a family for you to worry about, that what matters lies ahead of you, not behind? At twenty-one, can
you call yourself an adult? At twenty-one, can you feel
that living, when all's said and done, means belonging

to yourself, and that everything that came before was a kind of dream? Why try to forget it if it was a reasonably happy dream?

You wander through the city before and after your meetings with Lilota and the engineer who is helping to renovate some of the rooms in the old mansion. They're usually two- to three-hour walks (you love the steep little streets, the colonial passageways frozen in time, the ups and downs of La Paz: they make your heart pound, reminding you that it's there). But once or twice you've walked for even longer, like a rat trapped in a maze, or a madwoman, or, again, like a prisoner, only this time locked in the city, not the house. You tell yourself that it's in your blood, this trait of not being able to stay still, and find yourself wondering what else you carry in there. Another thing that's started to happen: increasingly you feel that your life can fit into a single sentence, or at least a few. You are the beautiful girl who entered into the bonds of marriage with a rich kid who hardly knows her. You are the housewife without a house, the unfeeling wife, the one who devotes herself to helping others with a friend from school to escape the guilt and the boredom, and to forget about her husband's frequent trips away (does he go directly to the mines, or does he have a secret life, a life that might explain his incompetence and apathy?). You are the fine young thing the businessmen try to seduce, the self-assured sibling who sees one of her sisters every once in a while and has lost all contact with the other, the one she never really got along with. You are the motherless daughter who never stops thinking about her father, half of the time hating him profoundly, and the other half admiring and loving him unconditionally. You are the woman who speaks to the people who turn up at the shelter, who is interested in what they have to say, who is weighed down by their stories, even though they tend to be quiet types, men and women who vanish as silently as they appear. You are the woman who remains a stranger to herself. The ex-depressive, the quasi-Bolivian. A pitiful sum, whichever way you look at it.

Something finally happens, at one of the German Club Sunday luncheons, to break the tedium: Reinhard, your husband's long-lost brother, turns up. He has an air of the family about him, but his features are more delicate and his gestures almost childlike, which makes him even more attractive. At first, everyone is cordial with him, acting as if they saw him every week. Your husband introduces you. "My wife," you hear him say, and you hate the way those words reduce you. You hold out your hand and tell him your name. It's an awkward situation, above all because he wasn't there at the wedding, and you don't know if that's because he wasn't invited or because he couldn't be bothered. Your husband never talks about him. "Another time," he replied on the one occasion you asked why you hadn't met him. You didn't push him for more answers—on the rare occasions that he did this, it irritated you. Over lunch the conversation becomes heated the minute they begin to talk politics. Reinhard is critical of the Revolutionary Nationalist Movement and its methods. He says it's not enough to give land to the Indians, and less meaningful still to let them vote ("Vote for whom?" he asks, when your husband challenges him. "Vote for which of the little white men exploiting them?"). He tells us it's brewing, that those of us present should hold on to our hats and our wallets, should be quaking in our boots. You've never heard anyone speak like this before—his words unsettle you. You feel dizzy suddenly and at the table they take it as a sign that at last you're pregnant. You know you can't be but don't contradict them. "I'd like to go home," is all you say. In the car your husband doesn't stop moaning. "Pretty easy, isn't it, to be a communist when your family's rolling in money," he says. "Not too hard in those circumstances. I mean, in those circumstances, who wouldn't?" He doesn't once ask how you are.

Three days later, tall and slim, energetic, handsome, your brother-in-law turns up at the old mansion. The shelter had come up in the argument at the German Club, his mother insisting that this was the way to do something; by doing it, not just talking about the need to do it. "There are people who actually do things for others," his mother had said, using you as one example, herself as another. Alongside his studies, Reinhard works part-time in a hospital a few blocks away from the shelter, and he wants you to know that you can count on him for anything, now or in the future. There's nothing defiant in his attitude, just a willingness to help. More than once he says you should tell his brother and parents if it makes you feel more comfortable. You ask him if he'd like to take a look around the facilities and he accepts with an interest you've never felt from your husband. As you tell him about the project, you realize you're proud of what you've achieved up until now, excited by all that's still to be done. Reinhard listens attentively, occasionally asking questions. He asks the people at the shelter things too, and even examines one of them, telling him to come and find him in the hospital, where he could do a proper consultation. How is it possible that he's your husband's brother? you ask yourself. How is it possible you don't recognize either of them in the other? Half an hour later he says good-bye, offering you his hand, not the kiss you would have expected, the kiss you were waiting for, the kiss everyone gives each other in this country.

Shortly after, you receive a letter from your father in West Berlin. He is still upset by the fact that you got married without his consent. "People don't marry so young these days," he writes in a messy, angry scrawl. "Monika, where did the adventuress go?" he asks (and how it cuts to see him call you by your name). Where did you hide the person who made him so proud? Where did you leave the woman who could have conquered the world, who was destined for great things? What did you do with the most gifted of his daughters? "I expected more from you," he signs off, and you read the sentence several times, convincing yourself that it really is there on the page. You respond with a few lines explaining that phantom fathers don't get a say in the fates of their children, and that this is what he had always been, that if he didn't know the first thing about anything, better to say nothing at all. It's just past ten twenty and your husband is asleep at your side. In the morning he'll leave again for the mines. You've been living together for half a year and are still strangers, and neither of you seems able to fix that. The promise of a different life continues to be nothing but a promise. Is it your father's words that have brought all this on? Minutes later, you tear up both of your letters and throw them in the toilet. Back in bed, as tends to happen, you end up thinking about the expedition. You think about your mother too, about how cruel he was to her, the rumors about him and Burgl, his and Burgl's betrayal, and all of this brings you back around to the side of hate. Were they already lovers when you met her? Looking back, were there signs that gave their affair away? You go over what memories you still hold but don't come to any conclusions. Yet it's the very possibility of your ignorance, the loathsome credulity that prevented you from seeing beyond what was in front of you that infuriates you more than anything that might have gone on. You could reread the diaries, look at the photos more closely. It was a decisive period, your time in the rain forest. You didn't find anything, never got to Paitití, but at the same time you found too much, every one of you. Without even going very far, your father found Burgl and Heidi her Rudi. And you, what did you find? Hours later, with that question still roving in circles above your head—"And you? And you? And you?"—your husband stirs at your side. You close your eyes and lie still, pretending to sleep. He takes a shower, gets dressed, and leaves.

# Trixi

The sixties were strange from the outset, strange and difficult, and back then, when they began, I was smoking at least two packs a day.

I smoked because I was anxious and bored.

I smoked before and after meals, on going to sleep and waking.

I smoked because my idea of happiness was smoking, sitting down or on my feet, standing still or on the move, although it's true I never did much like walking. The real walker was Monika, and there (and only there) I saw a similarity to Mama, who would also use any excuse to stroll around the city.

When the sixties began, Mama had been dead almost two years, from a cancer that caused her so much pain by the end that more than once she asked us to help her die. "Help me die," she repeated, in her sleep or awake, her lungs and spine and liver riddled with tumors, some big, others small. "Help me die once and for all."

"Ridiculous to think it would be any better here," she said to me one afternoon as the morphine kicked in. I didn't understand what she meant, but nor did I want to ask. We were alone in the hospital room where she spent her last weeks.

Even there she would ask me to hold a cigarette to her mouth, and I would, puffing away beside her. Mama was dying and we were smoking together.

Afterward I would open the windows and spray perfume on her so the nurses wouldn't notice. They did but never said anything.

Monika and Heidi paid visits. They couldn't handle the spectacle as well as I could, so they never stayed for long.

Together we managed to make Mama laugh.

Together we managed to forget why we were in that room.

But none of that's important. What's important is 1960, the start of a new decade, one that I was destined to spend alone. Back then I would try my hardest to remember Mama's face and never could. Sometimes I saw her in dreams, where we appeared identical.

I suppose her most obvious traits did live on in me.

In my phobia of insects.

In my fear of men's mirth.

In my constant need to smoke, although not the Astorias she loved so much and which always made my throat burn.

If I didn't have a cigarette between my fingers, a cigarette that I could put to my lips from time to time, I felt helpless. I shrank into myself, became even uglier.

That's why I smoked. And to fill Mama's shoes for the duration of those cigarettes, because it was when I smoked that I was most like her.


Recently back from a long stay in Europe, just months after we buried Mama, Papa bought some land out in the east near Concepción and went there with that Burgl woman to build a hacienda. Heidi, in turn, made an inverse journey back to Munich and disappeared from our lives.

I had just finished school and was living alone in our house in La Paz, having given myself a few months off.

I had never had a boyfriend.

I had friends, but not really.

I had sisters, although perhaps not that either.

Heidi least of all since she'd moved in with Rudi and had their first child. In a little over a year they had also set up their sports shop. She insisted I visit, stay with them for a couple of months. I could look after their little girl, they'd be happy to pay me a decent wage.

In April of 1960 I helped Monika raise money for the shelter. Not long after, I began working mornings there. Monika's husband offered me a job in his parents' import business in the afternoons and I began in the same role Mama had had years earlier.

There were strikes in the middle of that year, one after the other, and also armed conflicts in some mines in Potosí. Monika kept me up to date. She applauded the development, claiming that violence was sometimes necessary for the greater good. For some time she had been accompanying Reinhard, her brother-in-law, at his meetings (they'd grown close, he was often at the shelter), and it was there that she picked up the ideas she would then repeat over and over again.

"We're not just going to sit here with our arms crossed," she would say. "We have a moral responsibility to dismantle this dreadful machinery."

My sisters were changing: I could feel it all the time. I felt it even more strongly when, in September of that same year, they both announced they were pregnant, Heidi for the second time.

She made me swear I would help her when the baby was born, and I began to think it wasn't a bad idea to have a trip on the horizon. It wasn't bad, after months of hard work, to know I might go back to Munich and that I'd have a bed there and food and a salary for looking after my niece and nephew, something I would have gladly done for free.

It was around that time that Papa asked me to move into the apartment down at the end of the garden. He needed money and he wanted to rent out the house in order to finish building Dolorosa, his hacienda. Monika helped me, just as I had helped her three years earlier.

Together we took over a few pieces of furniture and three or four boxes.

It was all I owned in the world.

"I have less," she said.

"That's not true," I said, "and anyway, you're going to have a child."

We were on a smoking break.

There was a time when my sister confided in me, when she would tell me her secrets. Now it was increasingly difficult to know what she was thinking or feeling. The only thing I could tell for certain was that she wasn't in a happy marriage, hence my surprise at her pregnancy.

"How are things?" I asked, to save us from the silence.

Monika smiled and said they were good. I tried to find something of Mama in that smile but couldn't. Mama could be found everywhere but in that smile.

"Does it have a name yet?" I asked.

"I'm only two and a half months along," she said.

"All the same," I said.

"No. Not yet."

"You should start looking for one."

"Trixi," she said. "It wouldn't be bad if she had the same name as her auntie Trixi, if it's a girl."

She said it as a joke but I responded in earnest.

"If it's a girl you should call her Aurelia," I said.

"It's more likely to be a girl."

"Why?"

"Because we're a family of women."

"Hm," I said.

"Yes, exactly."

It was an unremarkable moment, just another afternoon, but I knew there and then that with my move one life would end and another would begin, at least for me. It was a fleeting conviction that made me nervous and happy at once. We're no longer foreigners, I also remember thinking—we have a past here.

I offered her the pack.

Monika pulled out a cigarette and lit it. I did the same.

We smoked in silence, looking at the garden where a good part of our last six or seven years had been spent.

Two weeks later, three months into her pregnancy, she miscarried. The sixties, the start of the sixties, were that more than anything: the death of Monika's baby. I want to believe that what happened later wouldn't have if she'd become a mother. I want to believe that the doses of horror would have been significantly smaller for all of us if that baby hadn't died inside her.

It is, in any case, a pointless thought, a foolish supposition.

II

# Inti

"My girl's godmother has told me about you lot," the old man said as he fed them in the living room of his hut on that first afternoon of December 1967. "I know those aren't your real names. I know who you are—everyone knows by now." He said, "Teaches at a school in the city, my girl's godmother. She says I have to help you, says you're fighting on our behalf." Inti and the other four listened to him in silence. The fifty thousand pesos President Barrientos was offering for their heads would turn anyone's life around. They knew it would be all too easy to lure them into a trap. "You can stay here. Me and my granddaughter will help you," the old man said. He must have been about seventy. People from the country died younger, died from all sorts of things, died without even realizing they were dying.

That night they discussed their situation. None of

them doubted the old man's good intentions or the hut's favorable location.

They agreed to stay.

Two nights later, Inti dreamt that they were surrounded by at least a hundred soldiers. "Let's dig a tunnel," Benigno said. "These people are going to finish us off." "Well, twenty of them are coming down with me," Urbano said. The military had mortar and machine guns and Barrientos himself was among them. He shouted something in Quechua. "He says he'll count to ten before opening fire," Darío translated with unusual calm. "He says he speaks as the Maximum Leader of the Honorable Republic of Bolivia." Inti couldn't understand how the old man had managed to betray their whereabouts if he'd never left the hut, and he was asking himself just this when the first shots were fired. He was woken by his own screams.

Darío was helping the old man's granddaughter peel potatoes. They both looked at him and, knife in hand, Darío told him they were making a peanut soup he wouldn't forget for years. The girl giggled beside him. The Cubans were outside, Urbano and Pombo helping the old man plow his small farm, Benigno keeping guard. Inti stood watching from a distance. None of them noticed him there. It was already seven in the morning. "Why didn't you wake me?" he asked Darío when he went back into the house. "You need to rest," Darío answered. His short haircut and clean shave had taken years off him. It was strange to see him, to see all of them, like that: men who would be indistinguishable from any other man in the street, despite their emaciated bodies. They had endured months of starvation and war, and it showed. They had lost too much, and it showed. Inti had been having similar dreams for months and it was always his own screams that woke him, just before the fighting broke out. He looked around for his diary. He wanted to make a record of these stationary times when the war raged on, the war between the living and the dead, but above all between the living.

In a hut occupied by five guerillas, an old man, and his granddaughter, it was silence that prevailed. Inti, the quietest among them, was grateful for it.

The closest neighbors lived more than seven kilometers away. "How far is the town from here?" Pombo asked on one of the first nights. "Twelve," the old man said, "along the main road to Santa Cruz." "It must be crawling with uniforms," Benigno said. "We'll have to go through the bush." "The Indians aren't on our side,"

Urbano said. "So what do you suggest we do then?" Benigno snapped. It had taken them weeks to break the line the enemy had formed around them in La Higuera. By the time they managed to withdraw there were nine of them, the last nine, but four more fell as they fled. Inti had led the escape—now he wasn't saying a word. Just beyond where they were sitting, the granddaughter knitted without taking her eyes off them. Urbano and Pombo didn't find it easy taking orders from a Bolivian, let alone one who hardly spoke, but they knew they had to obey him and acknowledged the good job he'd done in getting them out alive. "We'll talk about it in the morning," Inti finally ruled. "It's late."

He was still awake an hour later. Out in the bush you didn't notice the broken chorus of breathing and snoring. Now, in this cramped space, it was enough to drive you crazy. Lying in the pitch black, trying to sleep, he remembers his brother Coco on the Mamoré River and his first job hunting alligators. The future had seemed bright back then: the two of them were going to go far, be upstanding men. He thought about the joy the river brought them, about his brother's explosive laugh. Two years later, now in La Paz, they joined the union in the factory where they worked, and not much later the party. He wanted to fall asleep imagining that one of those snores belonged to his brother, that the next day Coco would be there when he woke up. At midnight he gave up—it was useless to go on trying.

Inti slipped out without a sound and soon reached the lookout post. Darío was smoking. He sat down at his side. After a while, as Darío began to nod off, Inti offered to take over while he went in and rested. "I already owe you God knows how many," Darío said. "You don't owe me anything," Inti replied. The cold made him feel more alive. As did being outside, by himself.

A plan to get back to the city was beginning to form in his head. He used the following hours to pin down the minor details. For the first time in months he was able to imagine himself out of there. They were already less weak, less exhausted, less dead, and soon all this would be a dream, he told himself. An infernal dream from which they'd managed to escape.


Two weeks later Inti and Pombo were swept up in the sounds of blaring car loudspeakers, voices intermingling, music pumping out of amplifiers on the shop entrances. It smelled of fried meat and savory pies and sweet, spiced *api*. It was chaos.

They were alone—the others were waiting back at the old man's hut. The pair would soon have to coordinate their comrades' escape too, but for now they had to

Rodrigo Hasbún

concentrate on saving themselves. The two of them were
dressed as Indians, in sandals and ponchos and chullo
hats. Inti told Pombo to avoid drawing attention to himself and then disappeared into the belly of the market.
These are the things Coco will never have a chance to
see again, he thought as he wove his way through the
heaving passages, the market women telling him they'd
give him a good price, inviting him to take a look, "Come
along, mister, no obligation to buy, we've got perfumes,
watches, trinkets, everything you could need right here."
The world had gone on, an overwhelming fact to digest.
He walked hurriedly, not looking at anyone but wondering what he would do if someone recognized him. He had
been awake for fifty hours. Just as in the worst moments,
it was pure adrenaline that kept him going.

They got changed on an empty plot of land and buried the guns and clothes, which they no longer needed.
Then they went into a restaurant and took turns to use
the bathroom. Everything felt strange: sitting down on
the toilet bowl to shit, their own image in the mirror, the
harsh tang of the toothpaste, the cold smack of the razor
against their skin. Dead men returning from the other
side, that's what they were. Dead men no longer afraid
of death.

After breakfast, they went looking for the LAB Air-
lines office and bought two tickets to Cochabamba. The

roads might be taken, but surely not the air. Four hours later they were boarding a plane. A few soldiers were traveling alongside them. The two of them sat in separate seats, pretending to sleep. They felt exposed without their guns. Without the forest for cover they felt like the easiest targets in the world. Nobody paid them the slightest attention.

Inti called an old comrade from the party from a public telephone on Aroma Street. Pombo stood waiting for him on the opposite corner, browsing a shop window but really only focusing on what was happening in its reflection. No one picked up. Inti tried another comrade's number. A little girl answered and he asked for her father. "He's not in," the girl said. "Who should I say called?" "And your mom?" Inti said, trying not to lose his cool and glancing out onto the street. In the distance Pombo was rubbing his eyes. Inti couldn't tell if seeing him calmed him down or made it worse. Pombo stood out with his dark skin. "Who's calling?" the girl asked again. "Manuel Silva," Inti said, and a few seconds later he heard the mother's voice come on. "You're already out of hospital?" she asked. "Yes," he said, "I've just got out, I'd like to see you." "My husband's not in," she said. "Call at six, he'll be back from work then." "I'll do that,"

Rodrigo Hasbún

he said, and hung up. He started walking, knowing that Pombo was trailing him on the opposite sidewalk.

There was lots of movement in the street, dozens of people to help keep them hidden. They had to remain calm. The military still believed they were in the forest and they weren't entirely mistaken—Urbano, Benigno, and Darío were still there. After several blocks, Inti stopped at another public telephone. He dialed the first number again. After the fifth ring he heard the voice of his old comrade. "It's Manuel Silva," he said. The other voice was silent for several seconds. "Manuel who?" he asked at last. "Manuel Silva, I've just gotten out of the hospital. Tonsils out, nothing serious." The other voice stayed silent. "I'd like to see you," Inti said.

A month and a half later, thanks to the cooperation of the Socialist Party of Chile, the three Cubans returned to their own country, where they were given a hero's welcome. Realizing he could be happy in the backcountry, Darío stayed on to live with the old man and his granddaughter. Now it was Inti's turn to get out.

The final stretch was going to be tough, but he felt as strong now as he had at the start of it all and he wasn't afraid. Along with two students who were also being followed, he arrived by car at the foothills of the mountain range and together they began the ascent up into the Andes on foot. It didn't take long for them to get lost on that snow-covered terrain. The other two gave up three hours later when their limbs began to freeze. Inti ordered them to carry on. "Come on. Fuck. We're nearly there," he shouted, more for his own sake than theirs.

When they arrived at the first village, they were met by three Chilean comrades. They were better organized than in Bolivia and transferred them that same day to Santiago. The two students had to be hospitalized immediately. Both lost several toes.

Inti spent the following weeks in Prague and Moscow. Finally, in the middle of June, exactly eight months after Che's death and nineteen after having gone into the forest at his side, he arrived in Havana.

From there they would regroup.

The battle had only just begun.

# Reinhard

Yes, in August 1964, I went to specialize in surgery in Freiburg, where I was given a decent grant. Some saw it as an ideological betrayal, but my options were few and this was without a doubt the best one. // Yes, almost immediately I began to live a double life. During the day I would go to the hospital to carry out my duties there. It was a grueling program, particularly the operations themselves. Death had become an everyday occurrence: an average of one in every four patients didn't survive. My other life, which began the moment I arrived home, was largely reliant on the news I received from La Paz, the city I missed and didn't know if I was to return to. // Yes, I kept everything my friends told me in their letters to myself. In more than one of hers, Monika asked me to translate statements. I did it at night, by this point more out of loyalty to her than any real conviction. Then, as instructed, I sent the translations to the members of a commune that maintained ties with Latin America. I didn't put my name to the translations. // Yes, every now and then I would pick up a nurse from the hospital, the sister of a patient, women I met in bars. I even thought I'd fallen in love with one of them. But it's no exaggeration to say that ultimately it was Monika whom I thought about more than anyone. I was twenty-six, and then, before I knew it I'd turned twenty-seven, then twenty-eight and twenty-nine, and sex was my way of holding on to my youth. In the moment with these women I would start to feel safe again, but a few hours later I'd invariably ask them to leave. How it was possible that someone who had never belonged to me kept on returning I don't know, but Monika was always present, watching me screw those other women, judging my false caresses, weighing up my desire and the frustration or satisfaction of that desire. Only the whiskey I'd got used to drinking every night helped me to regain a little calm. // Yes, during this time, guerrilla movements sprouted up all over Latin America, in Argentina and Colombia, Venezuela and Peru, but none of them caught on. After the guerrilla movement was defeated in Bolivia and everything went to shit, the news I received was increasingly disturbing. I learned that the minister Toto Quintanilla had ordered the amputation of Che's hands to send them to Cuba by way of proof that he was dead, and that Che's men had taken this as an unforgivably brutal act. I learned that four of the guerrillas who fought at his side had managed to escape and that there was another who'd stayed in the bush because he'd fallen for an Indian girl. I learned that both of them, along with the girl's grandfather, had been viciously executed and that she was six months pregnant at the time. I learned that President Barrientos died in an attack on his helicopter and that Inti, the only one of the Bolivians to survive in the end, tried to reassemble the men on his return to La Paz. I learned that Monika was now working closely with him. Lastly, just as I was about to graduate and take up a job in the same hospital where I'd done my specialization (La Paz would have to wait—it wasn't a good moment to go back), I learned she would be traveling to Europe for a few weeks and that she wanted to see me. // Yes, I hardly recognized her. She had short hair and her facial features had hardened, but the most significant change was in her eyes, which had lost all their warmth. We walked together to a restaurant I liked, forcing ourselves to chat about any old thing and recalling a few common friends. It was the same old same old: things had gone well for some of them, not so well for others. I asked her if she was planning to visit Heidi in Munich. She told me that it had been years since they'd spoken ("It's better that way," she said, and I couldn't help but think of my brother and parents), that Heidi didn't even know she was in Europe, that nobody else knew. // Yes, as we ate, Monika refused to touch a drop of alcohol and seemed more concerned about our surroundings than our conversation or me. She looked about her but was also clearly listening to everything going on in the room, no doubt trying to detect any signs of danger. There were none, at least none that I could tell. // Yes, according to what she told me when we went back to my apartment, some important people were involved in the fight. Just across the border a few days later she would meet up with Feltrinelli, the Italian editor. How easy to be the one who lays down the cash, I remember thinking, how easy not to have to lay down your body too. // Yes, in my living room she relaxed a little and every so often the Monika I knew rose to the surface. I'd spent years remembering this woman. She had never not been with me, this woman. From a few loose pieces of information I realized how indispensable she was to the National Liberation Army, which Che had founded a few years earlier and Inti now led. I learned that she loved the latter of these men (ten times more than she had once loved me, I told myself as I listened to her, a thousand, a million times more) and she felt that she had at last found her place in the world, a mission that made sense of her life. I learned that the years had not passed for nothing, that she was no longer the well-intentioned young girl I once knew but a diehard militant who traveled around Europe visiting communes and collecting funds. I learned—it was impossible not to—that now I really had fallen outside the circle, and that from the outside it was chilling to look in. // Yes, in spite of everything, in that moment I would have given anything to undress Monika, to bite her nipples and run my tongue over her, but I was aware of what we were and of what we no longer were, and I didn't so much as hint at the idea. At around three she fell asleep. I covered her with a blanket and went to my room. The woman I had loved more than any other in my life, that woman whose memory had tormented me for years, the woman who had left a permanent stain inside me was asleep in the armchair of my living room, and she was a stranger. // Yes, when I woke up, Monika was no longer there. She had left without saying good-bye. // Yes, of course: that was the last time I would see her.

# Trixi

None of us sisters was particularly lucky in love. You could say that. At least, that's what I tell myself. In the long term, love didn't work out for any of us.

Not even for Heidi. She and Rudi had four children and their shop did so well they opened several outlets and everything seemed perfect or nearly perfect for about ten years, until he got bored. For them it must have been a gradual change, but for me the news came as a bolt from the blue.

Rudi told her he was after new adventures and that he couldn't abide so much comfort. Heidi told him to do whatever he liked but to think about it long and hard first because there would be no going back.

She wrote all this to me in a letter. She told me that she still loved him, despite the various infidelities that had come out (they didn't matter to her, the sex was the least of it), but that she wasn't willing to end up like Mama.

She told me she wasn't afraid of being on her own. With four children that wasn't possible. She also said, though, that there were days when life seemed too much for her, and that it saddened her that we lived so far apart.

For the few months I'd stayed with them, I'd envied their life together. Heidi was radiant. The children and her husband brought out the best in her. It was even strange at first to hear her laugh so much.

"You girls aren't even aware of who you have for a father," Rudi told me one night as my sister put the children to sleep.

"What do you mean?" I asked.

"You're so unaware," he repeated.

I said nothing.

"He's a great man," he said, "one of the best photographers ever to come out of this country, a first-class explorer."

"But hardly a model father," I said. "Nor a good husband."

"You can't know that for sure," Rudi said.

I could be surer of it than anyone. I remembered Mama's endless waits, her delusions, and the final letdown. I'm not going to be unfair: I also remembered her from before, the good old days when she was at peace, and I remembered her clumsy Spanish, just the thought of which would set me off laughing wherever I happened to be.

Like right then, for example, in front of Rudi, in the living room of his house.

"What?" he asked.

"Nothing," I said.

When Heidi came back she sat on his lap, and my envy of her, of them both, returned. But a few years later he got bored.

You want the best for your siblings and that doesn't always happen.

You want the best for yourself and that's almost never possible.

With the exception of my grandparents, who now lived in the countryside and whom I visited on a couple of occasions during my stay, I didn't know anyone in Munich. The city was a museum in motion, an endlessly fascinating place, but my enthusiasm only lasted a matter of weeks. Afterward, I began to miss the chaos of La Paz, my life there.

It was a simple life, and remained so for years, above all on my return from months looking after Rudi and Heidi's children, of which there were just two back then.

I worked.

At the shelter, before they shut it down.

And for the import business, even though I left when Monika and Hans's relationship really began to go downhill. By the end (too protracted an end for such a farce of a relationship) they didn't even sleep in the same room.

She was now part of some sort of collective and from a certain point onward spoke of nothing but that. She tried to pass on her enthusiasm to me, but politics weren't my thing. They weren't my thing because all my energy went into making ends meet. Monika was still married to Hans, and although things between them were bad, money wasn't an issue for her.

But back to Heidi and Rudi: he ended up going off to live with some twenty-something-year-old Kenyan girl. His plans to set off on new expeditions had gone out the window after a first disastrous attempt. I guess he realized that sex and love were the only kinds of adventures he could still embark on.

Heidi got the house and two shops, and the business continued to go well for her. So well that, every now and then, she would send me a check.

From what I could tell, she also sent them to Papa. Around that time he suggested I leave my jobs temporarily to accompany him on a new expedition. He wanted to cross Latin America making a documentary, and he needed me to drive the Kombi he would rent. In return for my services he would pay me more than I was earning now, with the money Heidi had agreed to give him to finance the fiasco.

"But what's the documentary about?" I asked.

"Us traveling through Latin America," he said.

"I'd rather not be on camera."

"So don't go on camera."

"Why doesn't Burgl do it?"

"She's going to use the time to visit her family."

"I'm no good at driving," I said.

We were talking over the phone.

He was calling from Concepción, the nearest town to Dolorosa, the hacienda he'd built.

"Do cut the crap, Trixi," he said.

A month later we left. Three weeks after that we had an accident crossing a river and Papa lost all the material he'd filmed and I fractured my leg. It was the end of his cinematographic career. From that day on he wanted neither to film nor to take photos. He said he took the accident as a sign and that one must always listen to signs, that that's how he'd gone through his entire life and he had nothing to regret.

I refused to talk to him for some time. We were incapable of having meaningful conversations, but worse than that, he wouldn't let me smoke in his company, which made me sick. I hadn't been dependent on him for a long time. Knowing how to be alone was my one great achievement in life.

But anyway, toward the end of the sixties, Heidi was

an abandoned mother of four, I hadn't met anyone, and Monika (finally free of her husband) had ended up in an even worse situation. I gathered by word of mouth that she was now living with Inti, a guerrilla fighter to whom she never introduced me, a guerrilla whom I saw on the cover of a newspaper several months after I found out about the affair, in a large and rather sad photo. Despite knowing next to nothing about him, I knew who it was within a matter of seconds, recognizing his name, remembering it from some conversation or other. He had been her first and last love.

During an intense battle with the armed forces, the article explained, his own grenade had exploded before he was able to throw it, causing instant death. Given the circumstances, he had been buried immediately.

I sat staring at the photo for at least ten minutes. He was a handsome man. The article said he had a wife and children.

I wondered what role Monika must have played in his life and how much she must be suffering. It took me ten days to find her.

Seeing her confirmed everything. She looked devastated. I'd never seen her like that.

I hugged her and told her I was sorry.

I told her as well that I was worried, that enough was enough, that she could have been with him when he died.

"When they killed him," she snapped at me, pulling away from our hug. And since I didn't say anything, she repeated it, "When they killed him, Trixi."

"In the newspaper they said it was his own grenade that went off."

"They kicked his spine until it snapped. They smashed his head to pieces," my sister said. "For days on end, do you get it? They tore his ass apart with a stick. If you don't know the first thing about anything, better to say nothing at all.

"I'm sorry," I said.

"No, you don't even know what you're sorry for," she said.

"I'm sorry," I repeated.

Weeks later she left on a trip.

And I would say that was the last time I saw her.

# Dolorosa

It wasn't an easy journey. From Santa Cruz, Monika had to take the main road for four hours to Concepción, and from there it was at least three more hours of ruinous dirt roads.

She drove with the radio on. Her shoulders and neck ached—not even sleep could ease the tension. To make matters worse, she wasn't sleeping more than three hours at a time. She had nightmares and often woke up screaming and crying. Inti had suffered from the same problem, one more thing that united them. A cold shower usually brought her back to the world. Then she would do her exercises, eat something, and start work. She wrote messages, planned meetings. She thought up new ways to get funds. How much would her father know?

Monika hadn't seen another vehicle for half an hour. There'd be no need for her forged documents this time. She thought about last week's losses. They'd intercepted

Warmi, Miguel, and Juan in Cochabamba and a fight had broken out, only ending when Warmi's bullets ran out. Juan had managed to escape and Warmi asked Miguel to kill her so she couldn't be caught and subjected to worse by the soliders. Knowing she was right, he aimed at her heart and fired. When he heard them coming down the hallway he turned the gun on himself. He relayed all this to the press the following day. He hadn't succeeded in dying. Monika didn't know what the soldiers thought they would achieve by allowing him to make statements like that. Show how savage the extremists are? The girl, Warmi, was a Venezuelan trained in the GDR, he a Uruguayan. Juan, for his part, turned up dead two days later. They said he'd committed suicide. She didn't want to imagine what they must have done to him before killing him, or how much information they'd got out of him, or how much they'd get out of Miguel.

There had to be moles. That was the only way they could have caught up with them, the only way they could have tracked down Inti eleven months earlier. Sometimes the enemy is closer than you think. He sneaks in and disguises himself as one of you, as your most loyal friend. She would have to learn to spot him, before there were any more killings. In recent weeks there had also been deaths on the other side: the editor of *Hoy* newspaper and his wife, as well as one of Barrientos's ex-ministers.

On the radio, two broadcasters began commentating on a football match between Bolívar and Wilstermann. She could never get her head around how the country carried on as normal in the midst of so much terror.

She looked into one side mirror, then the other, and estimated she would be there around one. There were still a couple of hours to go. It wasn't an easy journey. It was even harder than she'd imagined.

Everything will be fine, Monika told herself. In the long run, everything will turn out OK.

Her father was with two men. She stood in the entrance of the house, which sat at the top of a hill. He was giving instructions, waving his arms dramatically while the others nodded. They were clearing a decent-sized patch of land and now they'd come up against some problems with a tree they were trying to cut down.

It would make the perfect spot. It was secluded, and not far from there was some uncharted land. That's what she was thinking when her father spotted her. He froze, convincing himself that what he was seeing was real, and then strode toward her, squeezing her tightly, instinctively, the moment he reached her.

They kept the conversation casual in the kitchen. In an attempt to ease the growing tension, Monika apologized for not having warned him she was coming and asked if she could stay for a few days.

"You can stay for as long as you like," was her father's response.

She thought he looked well. He had recently turned sixty-one but seemed considerably younger, despite his gray hair and beard. He showed her around the house. It was spacious and she was surprised to see how well kept it was. She was even more surprised to find one of the walls in the dining room covered in old photos. Her father had never been particularly given to nostalgia, a quality she had inherited.

"What are they doing outside?"

"They're making a runway. First we'll clear a decent strip of land, then level it, and then mark it out, and voilà."

"Why?"

"Well, you have to mark it out so that—"

"No," she interrupted, "why a runway?"

"Ah," he said. "I'm going to start selling my produce to an export business. The return's better, but they run a tight ship. The runway will speed up the traffic. And another thing," he boasted. "Every now and again my friends visit me in their light aircraft. They don't even come from far. The general's hacienda is a stone's throw from here."

"Colonel," she corrected him. "I didn't know you were friends."

"Have you eaten?"

Monika shook her head.

In his company she no longer felt in control. Her strength deserted her—she lost years in a matter of seconds. At thirty-two she regressed to being a teenager, a little girl who didn't know what to do with herself. She had to process this information, to accept that perhaps Philbrook was less safe than she had imagined.

She saw him go onto the terrace, where he called out a name. A moment later a small woman with Guaraní features appeared and greeted her submissively.

Nothing made Monika feel more uncomfortable than servitude. It was precisely servitude that reaffirmed in her the need to keep up the fight.

"Jacinta, what could you whip up for my daughter?"

"Whatever the young lady likes, Don Hans."

"What do you fancy?" her father asked her.

"Anything at all," she answered.


In the afternoon he gave her a tour of the land. He had large cornfields and hundreds of cows, chickens, and goats. They crossed paths with five of his employees along the way and she asked him if they lived here.

He said they had houses over to the east. To the west there was nothing, just wild bush that also belonged to him. He had two thousand hectares in total. She was impressed by how her father had managed to achieve all this on his own, by how he'd reinvented himself so convincingly.

They walked for hours, barely saying a word to one another. It was like being back in the rain forest, far from the world and the horrific things that happen in it. Monika was still thinking about one of the photos she'd noticed earlier on the dining room wall. She couldn't recall having seen it before and had certainly never owned a copy. It was taken at the end of the expedition, when Heidi and her mother had come along to catch up with them. All three of them were in the frame, as well as Burgl, Rudi, and her father. Now, without looking at it, she couldn't remember their expressions or what was behind them.

The moment they got back, she went to inspect the photo more closely. They were explorers but looked like guerrillas. They all seemed happy apart from her father, who was the only one without a smile on his face. She had revered him madly on that trip: his courage, his passion, his will.

"It's one of my favorite photos," she heard him say.

She turned and looked at him. Twelve or thirteen

years had passed since the end of the expedition. At times it seemed like double that, at others not even half.

"Ready for supper?"

Monika let out a laugh.

"What?" her father asked.

"I've only just eaten lunch," she said.

"Hours ago," he said.

"I'm fine."

"You look drained."

"I'm fine," Monika repeated.

"I'm not talking about the food," her father said. "I mean in general, I've never seen you like this. Jacinta has already fixed up your room. Go and sleep for a while."

She went out to the car for her rucksack and also took the opportunity to fetch the revolver she had under the seat. Back in her room, she slipped it under the pillow and took off her boots. She did a few exercises before getting into bed and woke up seven hours later. It had been years since she'd slept for that long, and she had to check her watch several times to convince herself that it had really happened. A few minutes later, without even realizing, she'd nodded off again.

When Monika left her room at six thirty the following morning, her father was already up and waiting for her at the table. Jacinta appeared with a glass of mandarin juice, offered her some oatmeal, and then, having served her some, asked how she liked her eggs. Monika was distracted over breakfast, absorbed in the twenty or so photos on the wall that summed up their lives.

"I tried to wake you up last night for supper but you were dead to the world," her father said.

He was trying to be nice. Their relationship had always had its ups and downs. There had been times when they had stopped speaking—when he made his relationship with Burgl official or when Monika got married—but there had also been moments of absolute intimacy.

She asked after Burgl.

"She's well," he said.

"Are you still together?"

It took a few minutes for her father to reply that he didn't know and that Burgl had been away for almost three years. They wrote to one another every fortnight and spoke on the telephone from time to time. For now they didn't have any plan to start things up again.

"And you?" he asked.

This was always the risk if they were going to play at being close again.

Monika thought about Inti. She recalled her days in Havana when she met him. She recalled the long walks they took together, the conversations, the sense of excitement. With her he had no longer been the reserved man all the others saw.

"I'm single," she replied.

"Your husband isn't a bad man, but he wasn't right for you," he said. "I knew all along that it wouldn't work."

Jacinta came in, rescuing them. She took away the plates, smiling, and a little while later they could even make out her voice as she sang to herself in the kitchen.

Her father had a few matters to attend to—they would see each other for lunch. Being alone often meant losing her sense of order, and that idea scared her. She decided to take a better look around the land.

"Is it quiet around here?" she asked Jacinta on her return.

"It doesn't get any quieter than this."

"You live in one of the small white houses, do you?"

"With my family, yes. I'm making *majao*, señorita. Do you like it?"

"You bet," Monika replied.

Back in her room she tried and failed to concentrate. The city and the war had vanished in less than a day: this place seemed like another planet. The enemy gets into your head, tries to convince you there's no sense in fighting, makes you believe you could abandon the fight, ignore what matters most, go back to your life from before. She hated herself for thinking these things, for her lack of seriousness.

As a means of self-preservation she thought about Inti, about his determination and how he spent months on the run. The news of the ambush had filled her with rage and pain but she hadn't let herself grieve for long. She also thought about her trips through Europe, years earlier. On her way through Freiburg during one such trip she met up with Reinhard. She'd intended to tell him she had been pregnant with his child, but in the end chose not to. He seemed a shadow of his former self, an utterly defeated man.

A feeling of desperation began to stir inside her. Monika didn't know how to fight it, had never known. She rooted around in her rucksack for her book. It was a collection of Che's essays and speeches published by Rowohlt. It felt strange reading them in translation.

Her father came back at midday. She heard him in the living room speaking with Jacinta in his stilted Spanish. Then Jacinta knocked on the door to tell her lunch was ready.

"Why are you here, Monika?" he asked her a few days later. They'd been walking in silence up until that point.

Now he had stopped and was looking at her. He wanted an instant reply. His old, intransigent ways were rearing their head again.

More than two years had passed since they'd seen one another. It must have been unnerving for her father, her being there. It was for her. It hadn't been an easy decision to visit him.

She was going to be direct, as direct as he was.

"I came to ask you for something," she said.

"I'm listening."

She took a deep breath and said she needed to ask him if he would let a few of her comrades live in Dolorosa for a while.

"I don't understand," her father said.

"They won't come near the house," she said. They would live in the bush. There, where they stood talking. The group was in urgent need of a safe place. Nobody need find out, not even his workers or the locals.

"A place for what?"

"To hide out for a while and train."

"The Bolivians have always been good to us," he said, cutting her off.

"This is for the Bolivians," she said. "There'll be new insurgencies. The guerrillas need to train in real conditions."

"Do you realize what you're asking me to do?"

"I'm asking you to help your daughter."

"Wars are fought in cities, Monika."

"They wouldn't stand a chance in the city."

"And in the middle of nowhere they would? Haven't you people learned your lesson yet?"

It was hard to believe her father was so well informed, that he was saying these things, that they were both keeping their cool.

"Let's go back to the house. It's getting late," he said.

"It wouldn't affect you in the least," she said.

"You don't know what you're saying."

"I'm saying a few comrades using your land wouldn't affect you."

"I don't want any part in your idiocies or your violence or your deaths," he said, now with another tone entirely, and glaring at her.

She had been naive to expect anything from her father.

"Let's go back. We'll carry on talking later," he said.

"I want to know if it's a definitive no."

"The time for these things has been and gone," he said.

"That's a no?"

"We'll talk later. Let's go back to the house."

---

Half an hour later they were screaming at each other in the living room. "You're nothing but a lackey to pigs in suits. A filthy fascist!" was the last thing Monika said before grabbing her keys, rucksack, and revolver from the room, and leaving without a word.

That scene would remain with him for the rest of his life. He would replay it obsessively in his mind over and again: his darling daughter insulting him, the sound of the car engine fading into the distance.

The next time he saw her was on a poster in La Paz. The army was offering a hundred thousand pesos for her, dead or alive.

# Monika

To feel nothing is to feel something? You spend years repeating it and now, as you hand over your documents, it happens again. No emotion, no memory: the watchword for any situation that calls for control. You cling to a single idea, to a few words, to that question that has reared its head again. You remain motionless, unflappable while an officer checks your passport and boarding pass. You know that any second now he will look up to inspect you (he looks up and inspects you), you know that you won't smile while he does (you don't smile, but you do hold his gaze fearlessly). "Did you like Bolivia?" he asks. Your name is Belén Hernández and you are a Spanish businesswoman who has spent the last three weeks traveling the country. "Yes, very much so," you say. "Academia or Tigre?" he asks. No emotion, no memory: this is what you think as you stare at him blankly as if you don't have a clue what he's talking about. You do: they're the most important soccer teams in La Paz, and you have no interest in either of them. "The glorious Academia, of course," he answers himself after a moment's pause, before handing back your documents with a smirk. You walk away, aware he's probably staring at your ass. In the departure lounge restroom an elderly lady warns you there's no paper. You thank her and lock yourself in anyway the moment she leaves. Most of the passengers have already boarded when you come out: it's safer to go last. Thirty-nine hours later you are in Prague's airport with a new passport they gave you at the Cuban embassy. You are now called Rosalinda Cabrera and you're en route back to Havana, your city of birth, after a flying work trip in the sister Socialist Republic of Czechoslovakia. Now nobody asks you a thing.


Three weeks later you are an Australian tourist calling the Bolivian consulate in Hamburg to request an appointment. You have a few queries regarding the visa for a group of travelers from your country. The secretary, a nice woman, tells you to come in exactly one week from now, at ten in the morning on the first of April: the consul general will be able to assist you personally. You tell her your name and that you'll be there, thank her, and hang up. Over the next few days you make sure everything is in order. You meet your contact in a crowded street where he hands you a small satchel with a Colt Cobra hidden in its false lining. Walking back to your hotel you feel as if every single second of your life has been geared toward preparing you for this. And yet your heart is thumping and at one point you feel like crying. Is there still time to back out? What would you do? Make peace with your father and take refuge with him in Dolorosa? Reopen the shelter? Give up your dreams and disappear in Europe, a continent to which you've felt completely unconnected for a long time now? You get to your room, put away the satchel, and lie on the floor to do some exercises. It is now, just when you need to let go of everything, that the memories rise to the surface. You want to scream, kick down the walls, head-butt the mirror: stretched out on the floor you take one, two, three deep breaths, hold in the air, let it out, and breathe normally again. An hour later you get into the shower and allow yourself a long time there under the water. You take more deep breaths. You mustn't abandon the present. The present is the cold water falling over you, your body shivering, the mission you are destined to complete, a mission that makes you happy. You shouldn't think too much, shouldn't leave yourself any room for doubt. You inspect the revolver. Its lightness pleases you. For the next hour you practice the moves until you have them down to perfection. Then you put everything away and go out for a walk.

You've only slept two hours but you're not tired. Until just now it was drizzling, but the sky is beginning to clear. "Victory or Death!" you write on a piece of paper ripped out of a magazine. You hide it in the wig that you carefully place on your head, and you think of Inti. A pair of thick-rimmed glasses go on next, and you look for the satchel, and you think of Inti. Your contact is outside. You get into the car and he asks if everything is OK. "Never better," you say. He seems calm, as if he did this every day. You don't know him well, and for a second or two you regret not having spoken more. He takes the Heilwigstrasse—you'll be there in less than seven minutes. You enter the consulate at five to ten. It smells of smoke and the secretary's sweet perfume. She remembers you and tells you to take a seat, the consul won't be long. There's a poster of Lake Titicaca on the wall facing you. You look away, concentrate on the small reddish mark on the tip of your shoe. It helps you focus on Che's amputated hands, on Inti's broken body, on that pig Toto Quintanilla, the man directly responsible for both of those things during his time in the ministry. You take one, two, three deep breaths. You exhale. You breathe normally again. Then you look up and see him: his mustache, his sideburns, his open smile. He comes toward you with his hand outstretched. He's greeting you. You pull out the Colt Cobra as you stand up and fire three times, aiming at his head.

It takes you half a year to get back to La Paz. You want to be there: there's so much to do. They send an Argentinian to look after you. He's twenty-four and you doubt his experience. You live in rough neighborhoods, never staying anywhere for longer than a week. Every screech of a car's brakes, every door that opens could be the enemy. You are constantly on the move. They'll only catch you if you stay still. You know they're coming for you. They believe it was you who did what you did. There are meetings, serious plans to destabilize the regime, a restored enthusiasm under the oppression. There is also sex with the Argentinian, an elemental sex that you don't understand but which helps you to combat the isolation. While you fuck, you remember your ex-husband, his brother, and Inti. You go back to being the body they used. That's how you see it: the body they used, the body the Argentinian now uses. The coldness is still there, you feel it inside you all the time. No emotion, no memory: this continues to be the watchword. To feel nothing is to feel something? Comrades keep falling. You want to help but the organization gives you barely any room to maneuver. They say that the CIA has gotten involved in the hunt for you, that there are posters with your face on them all over the country, that Toto Quintanilla was well regarded among the troops, and that they're going to move heaven and earth to avenge his assassination. You hate waiting. It takes you to places you would rather not be, to the alternative lives you never lived. You struggle most, though, with the feeling of uselessness (why have you come back if they won't let you do anything? what's the point in being here if it's as if you weren't?) and with being shut up. When you can't stand it any longer, regardless of the risk, you go out walking. Now, for example, it's seven in the morning and you've been awake for hours. The moment the Argentinian stirs, you tell him you need some fresh air. You put on your hat and poncho and take a look in the mirror. That's you now, you think, that woman on the other side is you.

# Trixi

Not only was it the start of a new year, it was the start of a new decade, and I wanted to move into both with one major resolution that would shape them. I had entertained the idea of finally finding myself a partner or moving to another city or country. But on the first of January 1970, from one second to the next, I made a resolution to give up smoking.

It was going to be the hardest thing I had ever had to do, but I needed a change and it made sense to start there.

I found cigarettes in the least expected places, loose and in their packs.

In the pockets of trousers I hadn't worn for years.

In plant pots.

Between the saucepans.

I threw them all in a black bag and went out onto the street. Having to wait two days for the garbage truck to come around would have finished me off, so I walked to an empty lot not far from my house and, having checked to make sure no one could see me, threw the bag away.

As kids we went through years of out-and-out trash wars with the neighbors. For every banana skin they threw into our garden, Monika, Heidi, and I would throw back three.

I remembered this as I walked back to that same house where we lived then, although for years now I had occupied just the apartment at the back, while family after family passed through the main building.

I found nostalgia served a purpose.

To feel that life had been worth it and to make the present fuller somehow. As I walked back, there weren't only those empty streets and that woman sidling through them alone. There was also the trash war that she and her sisters kept up for years with their neighbors. There were those sisters of various ages. There was the mother they more or less resembled.

That first of January was torturous.

I was completely desperate.

Sobbed like a madwoman.

Couldn't sleep.

By the following day it was even worse. My hands were trembling and my mouth tasted strange. My heart pounded uncommonly hard, as if trying to beat its way out of my body. When I finally managed to fall asleep I had nightmares. Maybe it didn't make any sense to give up smoking after all, if it made me so happy.

I had been teaching German for a while, private classes mainly, but also in the Goethe-Institut. I would soon be turning twenty-seven, and on the whole I couldn't complain, although lately I had begun to feel that I needed a serious change, something that would give me a renewed image of myself and of the world around me.

On the third of January I popped into several local shops, buying gum and candy when the only thing I really wanted in my mouth was a cigarette. That same day, at around midnight, I couldn't bear it any longer. It was a Saturday and there were places still open. I bought one pack and a lighter.

I crossed paths with three men on my way home. One of them made a heckle I didn't catch. No doubt some obscenity. The other two laughed.

There was still time not to go through with it.

I'm a superstitious person. I worried what might happen if I didn't stick to my resolution.

On Monday I would go back to work. On Monday I would begin the year proper, the loathsome seventies.

I picked up my pace and didn't stop until I got home.

———

A rumor was going around among the Germans that Monika was behind a few of the terrorist attacks that had happened in the city over those first few months. As a result, their attitude toward us changed. They shut us out.

Toward the middle of March they made it clear that I could no longer work in the Goethe-Institut. It didn't matter to me. The private tutoring paid better, so I didn't even give them the pleasure of asking them why.

Papa suffered more. His export suppliers put up millions of obstacles and after a while stopped buying from him altogether. His pride was greater than mine, and what really hurt him were the halfhearted greetings, the pleasure the others got out of talking about us. He'd spent years only occasionally leaving his hacienda, but now even those outings stopped.

"All that work to end up back where I started," he complained to me one day on the phone. He said he'd experienced something similar after the war, that they'd already made him feel like an outcast once, that back then they'd closed one door after another to him, but this time he wouldn't move an inch.

He wanted me to go and live with him in Dolorosa. What a name, I thought every time he mentioned it. In spite of everything, I was fine in La Paz.

It comforted me to be in the permanent company of

children and teenagers. I enjoyed watching how they steadily picked up a new language.

I had seven regular students I saw twice a week. There were also another three or four who would show up around exam time.

I made use of the time on my hands.

Truth be told, I didn't do too much.

I would gaze out the window.

Go to the cinema.

Once in a while I had tea with Lilota, Monika's obese friend. She worked in a hospital now but missed the shelter. We spoke about my sister in the past tense, her present still a mystery to us. We didn't even know if she was in the city.

At times I thought Monika was spying on me, that on certain days she was tracking my every move. At other times, as I walked back to the apartment, it occurred to me that I might find her there. We wouldn't say much to each other. Just hug for a long time and then jump onto the bed together and eventually fall asleep.

I missed our lives from years ago when we had just arrived and everything was new to us. I missed Mama. I still missed her. Maybe she had never stopped watching us. She would laugh at how little we'd achieved. She would laugh at how my attempt to quit smoking had lasted just three days.

Mine was a vague sort of nostalgia. I couldn't pin down precise moments. The few that did come back to me were our passage over by boat, the glorious Christmas of '55, and my first years alone in La Paz, when I was seventeen and everything seemed impossible. Now I was nearly a decade older and felt the same.

I didn't know how to ground myself in reality.

Reality was the newspapers that I began to flip through in the street (looking for Monika), the news broadcasts I heard on the radio (looking for Monika). Reality was the students whom I taught a language that they didn't understand why they were being made to learn. Reality was the people who got together and reproduced, and in so doing allowed the world's lies to keep on being spun.

My stomach began to give me problems. I couldn't hold in the need to go to the toilet and more than once I ended up shitting down deserted alleyways, cleaning myself with leaves or a newspaper I was lucky enough to find. Maybe to become an adult is precisely this: to be ashamed of your body and its emergencies and revolts, to be worried about that burning feeling you get after drinking coffee, to always fear the worst. All these things began happening to me at the start of the seventies, which must mean it was then that I became an adult.

This also happened: dozens of young men, most of

them younger than me, headed into the forest to start a new guerrilla war. The first thing I wondered when I heard was whether Monika was among them, if she too had gone to fight. Fight against whom? was the second thing I asked myself. Who the hell were they going to fight out there in the middle of the jungle?

In my despair I imagined that all this was my fault, that if I had only kept my promise of quitting smoking none of it would have happened.

I couldn't picture them.

Dozens of armed kids scrambling toward their death. Dozens of kids who would be decimated by the army.

And among them, perhaps, my sister.


Information was scarce and there was no way of knowing what to believe. Were there twenty of them? Fifty? One hundred? They had kidnapped two gringos not long before heading into the jungle, but apparently they'd already let them go. Nothing was certain if you didn't have a connection or acquaintance in the government, and I didn't have anyone.

I became glued to the radio, turning into that obsessive woman who scours all the papers from top to bottom at the newsstand on the corner of her street.

Some days I smoked up to three packs of cigarettes.

Anything that can go badly will, I told myself. Anything sad will get sadder.

Heidi was indifferent to the news. Half a lifetime had passed since she had seen Monika (who didn't even know her niece and nephews) and now they were total strangers. To my surprise, Papa didn't seem particularly alarmed either. He seemed hurt, as if Monika had committed a personal betrayal. He had high ranking military friends and told me he would find out more, but I knew that he was more concerned about saving face in front of them and that he wouldn't show any weakness, even in the most extreme circumstances.

Back then I didn't even know where Teoponte was. I didn't know who the Social Democrats were or what *foquismo*, the guerrilla strategies Che endorsed, really consisted of. I didn't know that among the communists there were both pro-Soviet and pro-China movements and that their differences of opinion were vast but that even so, both factions had come together this time, four years after the last attempt. I had never been interested in politics, and there I was learning all sorts of things that deep down I still didn't care about.

I cared about my sister.

I cared about the life and death of those young guerrillas.

"They're rookies," a military spokesperson stated.

"They don't pose the slightest threat to this country." "We'll have everything under control in a matter of weeks," another said.

I reread the statements they had made before entering the jungle a million times. I wanted to understand why they did it. I wanted the guerrilla movement to make some sense to me, a sense that corresponded to reality and not just to desire or stupidity. The only way to stay true to the Bolivian Revolution—they wrote—is to go beyond declaratory postures and take action, to assume the responsibility and the honor of taking up the arms that Che and Inti, together with many other comrades, left behind in the name of the National Liberation of our people. I didn't know where to position myself or what to do. In the midst of this confusion I turned twenty-seven.

Not long after that the first news came through.

Nine guerrillas fallen, the newspapers said.

Four guerrillas fallen, they said. And four more, and another seven.

And only at that point did Papa let me know that he had received word from Monika: he didn't know if she was in the country, but she was safe. He'd received a brief note, without much information, and completely devoid of emotion. It scared me to hear it (Papa read it to me over the phone, crying like a boy although he denied it when I asked what was wrong). The detachment in the letter was genuinely terrifying.

Over the next two or three months, close to sixty guerrillas lost their lives. According to the rumors, the majority of them starved to death.

The government officially called an end to the fight.


I saw my sister everywhere. Not a single day went by when I didn't see her. If the telephone rang, my first reaction was always to think it was her.

I bought a dog, and then another. I needed to feel that I had company, that someone was always there waiting for me at home.

I needed to find Monika and I didn't know how.

In the meantime, she multiplied.

She would turn up at the corner shop.

In one of the seats at the cinema I sometimes went to.

In the small squares where I walked my dogs.

I lost several students. Now there were just three, and my stomach was gradually worsening. Rumors still went around. People said my sister was a ruthless woman, a cold-blooded murderer who was single-handedly destroying the reputation of the Germans in Bolivia. Heidi tried to convince me to go back to Munich and help her with the children (who were no longer children) or to take over the running of one of her shops.

I knew I couldn't leave without finding Monika first, without convincing her to forget all that, to start a new life with me where nobody knew us. Our parents had done it, and Heidi too, in her own way.

They were the worst years of my life, and my only consolation was to convince myself that it was possible to start again far away. They were devastating years and my answer, time and time again, wherever I happened to be, was to make myself think like this.

Then I gave up.

It's not true that our memory is a safe place. In there too, things get distorted and lost. In there too, we end up turning away from the people we love the most.

*They see him in the distance. It's six in the morning and he's drinking his coffee as he waits for them, standing in the doorway of the house. Everything seems considerably more run-down than the last time they came, several years ago now.*

*Amadeo and Lucho, brothers by the same father and partners in their growing construction business, approach at the mule's pace. They're not sure what he wants from them this time. His appearance at the shop had been brief and disconcerting. It wouldn't be a tough job, he'd said. They should bring two hundred bricks and enough cement to lay them. They'd be done in a few hours. When Amadeo asked him to be more precise, the old man had said good-bye with a nod of his head and two or three words that neither of them understood. They'd worked for him as young lads, but it had been years since he'd come asking for their help.*

*Now, approaching the house, they notice that the thickets have grown, towering over it, and there are eight or nine dogs prowling around. From a distance they look like shadows, shadows coming together and then breaking apart in an inscrutable dance.*

*The brothers keep approaching in silence. Both are fright-*

Rodrigo Hasbún

*ened by the German's presence. His shabby appearance becomes clearer as they steadily climb the hill that leads to the house. Once they are forty or so meters away, he raises one arm and waves.*

*Two hours later they're shoveling earth from the rectangle they've marked out on his instructions. The German oversees the labor, standing a few meters away, surrounded by his dogs. They are his private guard, his kingdom, the only thing he has left beyond this house, which stands three hundred meters from the hole they're now digging.*

*And as for the brothers? Nothing, Lucho thinks. It's only midmorning but he's already hungry. Nothing, Amadeo thinks, and he wonders if there might be any money in the house, money that could change his and his brother's and both their families' lives. "Concentrate, Lucho," the old man says, and then he mutters a few unintelligible words and strokes one of the dogs' heads. Two others begin to fight. The German stands watching over the dogs and a strange silence falls, prompting the brothers to stop to see what's going on. The German seems lost, as if he weren't there. Maybe it's something that happens to all old people. What will I be like? Lucho asks himself, and he can't help imagining an enormous gut, a gut already beginning to show under his T-shirt. Amadeo is still wondering where the German keeps*

– 128 –

*his money. Close by the two dogs attack one another with growing ferocity. Wanting to finish soon, the brothers turn a blind eye to the spectacle and get back to work.*

*In a couple of hours they've managed to dig a hole one meter forty deep. The earth is soft from the rain. The German wants them to go down to two and a half. "That's pretty deep," Amadeo had told him that morning. "Two meters are more than enough, even one seventy, one eighty would be more than enough." Lucho nodded at his side with his head down. He struggled to look the German in the eyes. Something in them intimidated him: foreign countries, a daughter who, according to what people said, had been tortured and abused in the worst possible way by the soldiers, and two more girls who had left and never come back. "That's what men like him bring on themselves," the locals would say after a drink or two. "That's what happens to people who think they're invincible." "My mind's already made up," the German had said. "Two and a half meters will take us too long," Amadeo had insisted, "and besides, we don't have enough bricks." "There are more back at the house," the German had responded, his final word before they'd reached the spot where they would get on with the job. There he'd stayed for the next few hours. Was it what they thought it was? Was he making it for himself or because what was left of his daughter had been found?*

*"Let's eat," he says at midday, and without waiting for*

*an answer he turns and heads off in the direction of the house, supporting himself with a cane.*

*There are dirty plates everywhere and the place is foul smelling. Amadeo and Lucho, in their shock, can't help but exchange looks. Two dogs that managed to sneak in now sniff about under the old armchair in the living room. One of the walls is covered in photos but you can barely see them under the filth. Lucho wipes his finger across a few of them. In one, the German is standing at the top of a mountain. In another, you can see him operating a camera, young and strapping, a self-assured man. The photo that really catches Lucho's eye, however, is one in which the three daughters are smiling. There's something hypnotic about the way they stare into the camera and he can't take his eyes off it. Next to him, a distracted Amadeo wonders if it's even possible that there's money in a place like this.*

*From the kitchen, the German yells at them to come. They watch him take out two tins of tuna and another of corn. He hands them over for the brothers to open. A pair of worn-out motors, a tripod, and some cables lie discarded to one side. The piles of stuff make the place look small, even though they know it to be one of the biggest haciendas in the area. The German puts three forks and a packet of water biscuits on the table and sits down. "Eat up," he says, be-*

Affections

fore digging in himself. Both of them are ravenous, but they follow his lead cautiously. A few minutes later Amadeo tries to make conversation. He asks the old man how he came to live in that country, if after all this time he feels more Bolivian than German, what it is he most likes about Concepción. The old man's gaze remains fixed on the table and he doesn't respond to any of the questions. Only after a while do they realize that he has fallen asleep.

*How easy it would be to do away with the old fool,* Amadeo says to himself. Lucho thinks about how he'd prefer not to get old, and that with any luck he'll leave the miseries of this world behind before it comes to that.

When the German returns at three o'clock they've already finished digging the grave to his specifications. The dogs gather around him again and he shoos them away aggressively with his cane. How old must he be? At least ninety, maybe even a hundred, the hundred years of the century now coming to an end. They can't, nor do they want to imagine how much memory all those years equate to, or what might dwell there. "Now get lining the sides," the German orders. "We'll need water to mix the cement," Lucho says. "Bring some from the house," he replies.

There aren't many hours of light left. The brothers work quickly. They want to get out of there as soon as possible.

*The German's presence isn't good. He unnerves and disgusts them, so frail and dirty, already belonging more to the other side than this one.*

*After he pays them in the living room they go back outside, have a quick wash, and load up the mule. "My stomach's in knots," Lucho says to his brother. "Steak tonight?" Amadeo asks. "Steak und some stiff drinks," Lucho says. "I'll tell the wife to pull out all the stops and whip us up some fried cassava." "I'll tell Juana to do rice."*

*There's a fifty-minute journey ahead of them.*

*At least they're in good company.*

*They set off.*

# *About the Author*

Rodrigo Hasbún is a Bolivian novelist living and working in Houston. In 2007, he was selected by the Hay Festival as one of the best Latin American writers under the age of thirty-nine for Bogotá39, and in 2010 he was named one of Granta's Best Young Spanish-Language Novelists. He is the author of a previous novel and a collection of short stories, two of which have been made into films, and his work has appeared in *Granta*, *McSweeney's*, *Zoetrope*: *All-Story*, *Words Without Borders*, and elsewhere. *Affections* received an English PEN Award and has been published in twelve languages.